HARMONY

Interference

THE LAVERIAN EMPIRE

TANYA STEVERDING

Developmental edit by Kourtney Spak (kourtneyspak.com)

Edits By CrabeEditing@gmail.com

Book cover design by Sanja Gombar (bookcoverforyou.com)

ISBN: 979-8-987770-86-3 (paperback)
ISBN: 979-8-987770-85-6 (eBook)

HARMONY

Interference

THE LAVERIAN EMPIRE

CONTENT TRIGGER WARNING

Please understand that this book is intended for ADULTS only and is a Sci-Fi Fantasy romance novel.

I want to advise that while I try to write accepting and diverse worlds, the journey of good prevailing over evil will have moments that could cause some to feel triggered.

Please be mindful of your mental health. Read only if you are emotionally prepared for triggering content.

Reader Discretion is advised.

Death of family, violence, slavery, sexual assault is implied, war, foul language, sexual content, kidnapping, pregnancy.

If you feel you can continue to read this spicy romance, I hope you truly enjoy this adventure into Harmony's worlds.

All of you are very much appreciated.

Your humble author,

Tanya Steverding

This book is dedicated to my
family and friends:

To my Grizzly for being my bond mate and always
supporting my dreams. I love you always.

To my children, who inspire me and give my heart a reason
to dream.

To my parents who will always be my biggest fans.

To my friends where, family doesn't end with blood.

Your sisterhood and brotherhood have always lifted me up
when I needed you most.

I could not create and write these adventures without all of
you giving me your love and magic.

CHAPTER 1

Darah

Growing up in the bible belt of East Texas, my oddness stood out. I had this way about me where I pick up on other people's emotions. I read my tea leaves and listen to my gut, my intuition. I guess you'd say I am an empath.

Sometimes, I'd even get a vivid vision when I get touched. My mom says I am gifted. And that I get it from her grandmother's side. I have always been a misfit, and growing up here in the bible belt hasn't always been easy for me. My younger brother Jason had made life here so much easier since he took up for me a few years ago.

When I was at our town park, I was reading my book about sparkly vampires under a nice and cozy shady tree when my brother and his jock pals walked by.

"Look, that's the freak my girlfriend was telling us about. Be careful! One look, and she'll hex you," Clayton said, mocking me.

I had ignored them as usual, but it was the first time my brother ever witnessed anyone messing with me.

"Watch your fucking mouth! You ignorant son bitch!" Jason went on a rant as he gave Clayton an upper-hand punch. Jason knocked him flat on the ground. Clayton was a wannabe rodeo cowboy and football jock. His giant belt buckle caught my eye when he tried to scoot on his ass to back away from Jason's towering form.

"That's my sister, and she is not a witch! You will respect her, or I will put my own hex on you and be your worst fucking nightmare! Besides, she can last eight seconds longer on any bull in this town than you could ever dream of, Clayton. Hands down, Darah can out rodeo, hunt, and fish you anytime. She is more cowboy than you can ever dream to be, and she is a lot prettier doing it, too." Jason spits his chew on the ground next to Clayton's frazzled face.

"Just because she is so talented doesn't mean it's magic, you asshole! No one disrespects my sister." Jason stared down the other two dudes, helping Clayton off the ground.

"You owe Darah an apology. Now!" Jason demanded.

I was scared, my heart was pounding. I had never seen my brother that mad or violent before. I was embarrassed too, my face turning red, I could tell by the heat rushing into my cheeks.

"Jason, it's no big deal." I tried to say when my brother cut me off.

"Darah, it is a big damn deal!" Jason glared at his friends.

"He's right, Darah. I am sorry for offending you. I was wrong, and it was childish. I don't know you, and I had no right to be that mean to you. I am sorry, and I hope you can forgive me." Clayton groveled, looking sheepish under my brother's angry gaze. Clayton didn't look me in the eye as he dusted his wranglers off, his eye was swelling, turning red before my eyes.

"It's all good, Clayton. We are good." I insisted, ready for them to leave so I could shake off that whole ordeal.

"I'll meet you at the field in a minute. I need to make sure my sister is truly okay." Jason dismissed his pals as they walked away. If they were dogs, their tails would be tucked between their legs.

"Darah, I am so sorry he said that shit to you. I had no idea you have been bullied like this." Jason sat next to me, truly upset on my behalf.

"Stop being such a big little brother. You didn't need to go that far. I am a big girl. I am used to ignoring them. I can't believe you told them I can ride bulls, you liar." I laughed, trying to defuse his tension.

"Well, you can out-hunt or fish him. Clayton is such a showoff, but he has no real skills. He's getting to big for his britches if he thinks he can treat you like that. You are more cowboy than he can ever be, even if the bull riding was a white lie. He's an idiot. Now that I am in high school, these fools better stay in check when it comes to you, or I will put them in their place." Jason's eyes turned from anger to tender as he really looked at me.

"Darah, you are my big sister. I hate that these asshats don't know you like I do because they would all know that you are unique and wonderful. I am proud of you." Jason got up, dusted off his jeans, and gave me his Hollywood-worthy smile with those sweet dimples.

"I love you too, little bro. See you tonight."

After that day, Jason and I had a more grown-up relationship. I still kept it playful, but he truly changed my life. He protected me, and it wasn't long before I was left alone. I will always love him, but for that moment, it will always be a moment close to my heart.

Shaking off that pivotal memory, I returned my thoughts to the present. After taking a couple of years off school to work, today was the big day. I graduated high school two years ago and helped my parents pay for my brother's sports stuff. He was a big-shot football player in this town. He was about to be eighteen. I was now twenty-one and have finally gotten into college.

My parents and brother drove me from our East Texas town five hours to Austin to drop me off.

"Oh, Darah, I am so proud of you." My mom hugged me tightly. My dad then pulled me in for a hug.

"Darlin, this is just the beginning. You have the world at your fingertips." He gave me a sweet kiss on my head.

My brother Jason hugged me.

"Get me tickets to a University of Texas game and make friends. Tell the pretty girls about your hot younger brother." Jason said with a wink.

He was seventeen going on thirty, and some days, I think he was more grown up than I was. I doubt I would need to tell any pretty girls about him. They tend to swoon over him naturally. He dreams of playing football for UT, and I am sure he will have his pick of colleges.

"Dork," I said as I released his hug. I waved goodbye and watched them drive away in my dad's old Dodge truck.

"I hate city traffic, "my dad complained as they drove off in his old red Dodge Ram truck.

I was so happy and so hopeful in that moment. I am nervous about adulting alone, but I was here! I was finally doing it.

I turned and went up the stairs to my new dorms, just a bus ride away from my college campus and the beginning of my future. I opened the door to my very first independent home, well, at least until they assigned me a roomy. I had a couple of boxes of my stuff on my twin-sized bed. It was not much, but it was all I needed. That nervous excitement had me humming in delight. This was all new and extraordinary to me.

My cheap cell phone rang, distracting me from my plans to unpack. It was Jason calling me. My heart sank. He just left. Why was he calling me? My anxiety peeked, but I brushed it off and answered.

"Miss me already, dork," I said to my brother as I answered.

"Darah . . . it's bad." I heard sirens as Jason, weak and wheezing, said, "I love you." In a croaked whisper.

"What? Jason, answer me! What happened?" I heard the noise of people in the background and sirens as I cried into the phone, trying to find out what was happening. I felt utterly hopeless and terrified, waiting for answers.

Eventually, after what felt like forever, a first responder picked up Jason's phone.

"Hello." He said in a deep voice.

"Hello, hello, I am Darah, Jason's sister." I rattled out with nerves.

"He just called me. This is his phone your talking to me on. Please, tell me what happened. Is my family, okay?" I asked frantically.

Ma›am, there›s been a car accident on IH-35 northbound, there is a pile up of vehicles here, I am a first responder, we are sending your family to the Saint David South Austin Hospital. Please meet your family there, Ma›am.»

The click of the phone hanging up sent me into a panic. My face was numb, my ears rang, and dread swallowed me whole. I ordered a taxi with my shaky fingers. To take me to the hospital.

Saint Dawn, "shit!" what was it? Saint David, that's it, remember Darah, Think! I chastised myself.

Saint David, Austin, I kept repeating until I got the ride ordered.

"This can't be happening!" I told myself as I traveled in a cloak of fear to the hospital. I was suddenly in a living nightmare.

I waited in a state of shock at that hospital, pacing in the hall outside the seating area that I was directed to. Finally, a doctor approached me and took me to a private room. My heart sank. That can't be good. Private rooms to talk can't be any good. I panicked. I felt the doctor's dread as he faced me.

"Ma'am, your family is John Davis, Dana Davis, and Jason Davis? he asked as he read the names off of his notes.

"Yes, sir, please tell me they are alive," I begged with tears, fearing my radar was picking up the wrong message.

"Unfortunately, ma'am, they were found deceased at the scene. We have a counselor available . . .

"All three of them? Are you sure? Can you double-check?" This had to be a mistake. This couldn't be real.

"I am sorry ma'am all three are confirmed dead, they have passed away."

"No!" I cried as I ran away from him and out of the hospital. I ran into a new, unthinkable reality. One where I was no longer myself, just a shadow of who I was meant to be.

Grief had taken my whole heart and left me empty and alone. The little money I had saved was gone. I used it to cremate my family. I couldn't even afford to buy a permit to spread their ashes, much less get a headstone or plot. I chose to spread their ashes illegally at the botanical gardens in Austin. I asked, but it wasn't allowed.

I like the Japanese garden part of the botanical gardens, so I spread them there, and I go there to visit them. My parents had no will. The rancher they rented from quickly moved a new ranch hand and his family in. I couldn't get back to East Texas to sort through their affairs. My brothers coach packed up our trailer and stored our stuff in an empty Conex cargo container on his property, he said I could get it anytime. In the meantime, he would keep it safe.

Paying my rent after all the expenses of the funeral cremations was just not a possibility. I was in no shape for school or work. With the last of my money, I bought a tent and moved to the streets. I needed to grieve, pull myself together, and find a job.

I woke with a start, I looked around the tent I was sleeping in, trying to calm my pounding heart.

I wiped the sweat off my forehead with the sleeve of my sweatshirt. Then I grabbed my half-drank bottle of Gatorade and finished it off. Taking a deep breath, I settled back into my sleeping bag and tried to fall asleep again.

Even though I wasn't in the accident, every time I dreamed, I saw it as if from my brother's perspective. I could see the metal crushing in like a tin can, the glass shattering, smell the smoke of the damaged engine and the road tar, the taste of copper blood was the worst. I have relived that event nightly since the crash.

My brother's last memory was imprinted into my brain, a miserable way to be haunted by him. Guilt and grief were are all I knew. I was struggling to be better. To be what would make my family proud of me.

It had been six months, but it was all still so raw. I knew I needed to stop this wallowing and get myself right. I felt them watching me, and I know I made them sad.

I was gifted an annual gym membership as a farewell gift from the rancher's wife, Miss Anna. She wanted to treat me but told me to keep it between her and me that she got me the membership.

It was a huge blessing because I use my gym pass to take showers. I excel at camping, hunting, and fishing. I can work on a ranch. Getting dirty is what I do, but I need my daily bath. It›s just a thing for me to get clean.

My membership was about to expire, though. Being homeless was just not much of an option anymore. It was time for me to pull myself up by the bootstraps. I needed to start a job hunt and get off the streets.

I tried to move my tent daily and avoid the homeless camps. I wanted to grieve alone. I sang for money to eat and get by. My gut kept telling me that a change was in the air, and my morning tea leaves kept showing me stars.

What good was any of these signs when I had none to warn me about my family's accident? I could easily pick up on others, but my so-called gifts were just shit when it came to sensing things too close to me. Most of the time, I still get a sense that things get dull when it comes to me or those close to my heart.

Deciding sleep wouldn't be happening, I unfurled myself

from my sleeping bag and began to pack up my tent. I put my tea, snacks, essentials, and an outfit in my backpack. I grabbed my guitar case and hid my tent and stuff for camp. It was dark just before dawn, and I walked to the gym.

The sun came out, and the streets were getting busy with the morning commute. The smell of the city makes me home-sick for the ranch and East Texas. I soaked in the hot tub at the gym to ease my stiff body. Sleeping on the ground was difficult for my stiff back.

I was clean- Thank God for the little things. I wanted to start a job hunt today.

I walked through Zilker Park to watch the morning runners and see the water roll by in Barton Springs. I was walking to the botanical gardens when I took a moment to sit in the grass and pray for the first time in a long time.

If there is anything out there, please help me find my way.

A black lab ran past me after a ball its owner threw. I Stood up and went across the street to the botanical gardens to spend some time paying respect to my family. I snuck in again. Security will throw me out if I get caught. This time, they might even call the cops on me.

It was pretty much empty that early in the morning. I liked to watch the Koi fish swim around in their little world of water and lily pads. I stepped over stones in the pond when I heard a man yell.

"Hey! You there, stop right there!"

I jerked back and lost my footing, falling into the Koi Pond. The cold water surrounded me, and my heavy pack sank me. I barely caught a breath to hold before I went underwater.

My ears rang, and I felt myself being sucked down fast. Sinking deeper into the darkness, I didn't think the Koi Pond was this deep. I felt like I was going to drown. I was sinking into a dark deep water I could no longer see any fish or plants and not even the light from the surface anymore.

Just when I was about to gulp in a lungful of water, suddenly, I was pulled out of the darkness, and as I surfaced, cold air hit my face.

As soon as I got a lung full of air, I expected to see that guard. Instead, I saw a pastel furry face hissing at me and hopping off. I frantically pulled myself on the bank of the stream I was in, my guitar case still in my hands and backpack weighing me down, which made my efforts slippery and awkward.

I was officially terrified. I was surrounded by tall pine trees and a stream running steadily by. The crisp air made me tremble. I stood up to evaluate myself and this situation. With teeth chattering, I was officially scared.

My heart was pounding, and I hit my knees and opened my case, trying to pour the water out of it and save my guitar. I turned my guitar over to examine it. It was worn from when my mom had played it but mostly dry. My mother gifted it to me when I graduated high school. I couldn't lose it, too. Nothing was making any sense! My guitar was the only tangible thing that reminded me of my family. Seeing it gave me a small comfort that I needed in this craziness.

The smell of forest, moss, and leaves registered in my nose. I looked up, and I saw tall, dense trees. The humidity and heat of Austin were gone, replaced with a cold that gave my wet body chills.

"What the Hell?" I said to myself. Turning in a slow circle, I realized I was no longer in the botanical gardens. I was also not in Austin anymore, not with this chill. Had I lost my mind? This wasn't possible. It couldn't be real.

"Okay, Darah, get your shit together," I said to myself.

My heart was pounding so hard I heard it beating in my eardrums. Cold seeped in as I continued to shutter, looking around to figure out what kind of trouble I got into.

"It's like I fell into the Twilight Zone!" I mutter through chattering teeth.

CHAPTER 2

Darah

Laverian

I stripped off my wet clothes, pulled my things from my backpack, and laid them out to dry. I gathered leaves and fallen tree limbs and prayed my lighter worked.

"Oh lord, thank you, Jesus! It's colder than a well diggers ass in January" I said out loud as I made a fire to warm up and dry my clothes things I had in my pack.

I checked my body. I didn't see any injuries.

Am I dead? I wondered.

I put on my jeans and sweatshirt. My dirty outfit was in a grocery bag from showering at the gym. This was dryer than everything else. They were dirty but dry; I could live with that. I kept my tea leaves in a Ziplock bag. The tea looked like it survived the dip with the fish. Thank God for the little things.

My fire was burning out, so I packed up my damp things. I need to move to find shelter and figure out where I was. It was getting colder, and the light dabbling through the trees was fading. I felt like I have lost my mind. None of this makes sense to me. Survival mode has me just taking things one problem at a time. I got dry. Problem one was solved. Next, find shelter and figure all this out.

I climbed a tree to see if I could get a sense of direction. The sap and pine needles made my climb difficult with the lushness of the trees. I manage to get far enough up the tree to peek at the sky.

"Holy hell! Well, hush my mouth!" I blurted out as I saw two moons rising and the sunset colors set against a light purple sky.

I gripped the branch so hard my palm rubbed raw on the bark. I climbed down before I lost all light. I was stumbling through the woods as it got darker and colder. My shoes were wet and had that annoying squish with every step. I was incredibly loud with my stride and leaves underfoot. The sound of this forest was way off. Muffled and stale, no animal noise, not even a bird or squirrel. Not the buzzing of nighttime insects like cicadas. I was so used to hearing back home. It was eerily silent. Nothing seemed right.

There's no wind, just me disrupting the air with my breathing and footsteps. Like I was a ghost just strolling through the woods in another dimension. Maybe that's the answer. I drowned, and this was some kind of purgatory. The ringing in my ears increased, so I could no longer hear my heart pounding.

I was going to be madder than a wet hen if I had gotten sent to hell or purgatory. I huffed at the air.

If I was dead, I wanted my family. Where the hell was I? I stomped my foot like a toddler throwing a conniption fit. I felt miserable, too miserable to be dead. I heard a voice inside my head. A woman's voice.

'Darah, do not fear I am . . .' the voice faded out. Great! Now I heard voices.

I had officially broken my brain. I was on the crazy train. Maybe it was just my nerves getting to me. I felt like the porchlight was on but nobody was home. I just didn't understand a thing that was happening to me.

I saw movement in the shadow of a tree, so I shut up and stayed still, waiting to see if I was now seeing things, too. Fear kept me frozen. After a moment, I sank to the ground to sit and wallow. I drank water from my bottle. I fished in my bag for a granola bar. The chocolate chip was a bit soggy, but my stomach was cramped in pain as I unwrapped my snack.

I moaned as I chewed the first bite. I put the wrapper back in my pack and noticed a familiar little furry face peaking at me. Maybe a rabbit or a cat, I don't know. Whatever it was, it looked unique. Was it dangerous? I wondered.

"Hi there little dude, did I scare you before when I came out of the water?"

The furry thing hopped a little closer to me.

"Yeah, I am sorry about that. If it helps, I am scared, too." I tried to soothe the thing.

It felt curious about me. Good, at least it didn't want to attack. The creature had Something soothing about it. My gift sent me a sensation of emotion coming from that furry creature.

That pastel-colored fur ball was fascinating, reminding me of cotton candy from the fair with its pink and blue hues.

"You hungry?" I asked it as I threw a little piece toward the furry creature.

The rabbit cat-looking thing picked up the treat with its paw and ate it happily.

"Glad you like it," I said through my mouthful.

Maybe I drowned and I was in a coma now, this all must be a dream. This creature in front of me can't really be real. Can any of this be real? The lush growth around me makes it difficult to maneuver. I was sitting on a fern, I think. I lean back to gaze up.

"Owe! I yelped as I leaned back on a thorn, stabbing my hand.

The cotton candy-colored rabbit cat got startled and

jumped away from me. Death wouldn't be this miserable. If I were in a coma, would I feel this pain? I was going with my coma theory because that rabbit-cat thing is glowing now that I was startled. I'd like to think if I died, I'd be with my parents and my brother. Sadness wells up in me as I fought back tears and rub my wounded hand.

Who knew I had this kind of imagination? I shook my hand, trying to calm the sting from the thorn that got me. I fished around in my pack to get another granola and held it out to the creature.

"Sorry, pal, I wasn't expecting that either. I did not mean to scare you.

The cotton candy creature hopped up to my hand that held out the granola bar, sniffing with his little wet nose. I broke off another piece, and he took it from my hand and suddenly jumped in my lap, letting me pet his silky soft fur while it ate.

"You are a friendly one, aren't you?" I crooned. I felt warm and cozy with this cute fur ball comforting me.

"If you are just in my head, I will call you Candy since you look like a swirl of blue and pink cotton candy."

Candy must have liked it since it was rubbing his fluffy head all over me like a hug. Did I hear this thing purr? I laughed, a real, genuine laugh. I haven't laughed like that since before the accident. I must be hysterical.

"Candy, do you know your way around this forest? Because it is darker now and I am cold. These wet shoes are driving me insane. I might follow you down your rabbit hole if we could get warm there. I am cold and desperate here."

Candy just rubbed up against my hand, ignoring my desperation. Something about this fur ball made everything less scary. But I needed answers, and I needed to move. I put Candy on the ground and stood up, dusting myself off, not that it helped much for the mess I was.

"It was nice to meet you, Candy. You be safe now." I said as I hefted my backpack on and reluctantly took careful steps.

I held my guitar case with a slight tremble in my nervous

hands. I only had a small flashlight. Luckily, it was in a Ziplock bag with my change and pens, which I randomly stored there. Thankfully, it still worked. It's just a gas station pocket flashlight, so I was unsure how much juice it still had.

Things always look so ominous at night. Goosebumps covered my flesh, and my sloshy footsteps and breathing were the only sounds I heard. Candy was keeping pace with me somehow. It could move silently, I guess it wanted to stick with me a for a bit. I was not going to complain. I liked Candy's presence. My light landed on a pile of fallen trees, and I saw natural A-frame.

"It's not a hotel, but I might be able to work with this," I told Candy to calm my nerves.

I used a stick to rake out the leaves and debris under the logs. I made a fire and settled myself in this nook of trees. Candy came and snuggled up to me. I don't know how I managed, but I fell asleep to the tune of Candy's purr and chuffing sounds.

It was a rough night. The morning cold seeped into my bones, and my sweatshirt and jeans were damp with morning dew. If it wasn't for Candy lending me heat, I am not sure I would have been able to wake up.

It was starting to get light out, but there was a fog, so I couldn't see much as I opened my eyes. I decided to crawl out of my hole and move. Maybe blood flow will help ease the ache of this cold and revive my numb limbs.

As I stood up to stretch, I saw a blanket of fog covering the forest floor. The mist only came up to my knees. I might find this all more beautiful but appreciating anything through my chattering teeth and this gut-clinching, uncomfortable cold was almost impossible.

I peeled my damp jeans down so I could pee. Miserable is an understatement at this point. I saw Candy's movements under the fog as it dispersed the cloud. I watched it head out before me, passing a few trees. I was deciding if I should follow the fur ball as I buttoned up my pants when a shadow of a big arm shot out from behind a tree holding a net and swooped up my Candy.

Candy's fur started to glow as it hissed and tried to escape. Its fluffy tail was caught in the net's web. My adrenaline kicked in, and I stormed towards my new friend, Candy.

"Oh no, you didn't. I am gonna tan your hide, you grabbed the wrong fur ball today, Mister. That baby is mine!" I grabbed hold of what looked like a hand-woven fishing net and yanked.

I turned the corner of the tree trunk and found my five-foot-two face smooshed into the hard-muscled bare chest of a . . . What the hell are you?»

I startled and jumped back, still holding tight to my end of the net. I looked up and up until I met the black eyes of a dark purple man with ram-looking horns. He was dressed in shorts only and had leather-style boots. His bow and quiver were wrapped around his shoulders, and tribal tattoos marked up his arms. He had long black hair braided up.

When our eyes locked, the shock on his expression changed. Goose flesh rose all over me, a humming in my ears started, and my heart was pounding as a throb started throughout my body. I was insanely attracted to this demon-looking man. I saw the need in his black eyes, bringing me back to my senses. I was suddenly nervous and unsure of what to make of this unknown male before me.

I had officially lost my mind. Shaking off my desire. I yanked on the net again. This time, it came freely to me. I reached in and pulled Candy out of the net, helping untangle its foot and tail.

The huge purple male with horns gasped in shock.

"Well, you are definitely a boy. I am sorry I gave you a girl's name, but who cares? Boys can be Candy too, I suppose." I snuggled Candy close, kissing the top of his furry head. I tried to soothe him as his pastel glow grew dim, and he started to purr, licking my neck with his scratchy tongue.

I ramble when I get nervous. Candy snuggled into my

neck, thanking me for rescuing him. The big, bulky male slowly moved around me, inspecting, and sizing me up. Candy growled again and hissed at the man when he walked behind me. I turned to face him.

"Look! Candy is my fur buddy, so you can't have him." I said with as much dominance as I could muster. I was scared shitless at the alien male in front of me. Not just because he was purple with horns. Mostly because he was probably the sexiest male I have ever been attracted to.

I had to collect myself and focus on saving Candy from the sexy man. Sexy doesn't automatically mean this guy is safe.

I started walking backward away from the man. The male did not seem to want my Candy anymore. He looked at me like I was prey. "Fuck." I whispered as his hungry eyes melted my core.

The blanket of fog still hovered over the forest floor. I must have drowned, this had to be me in a coma, because glowing pastel fur rabbit cats don't exist, Sexy purple horned men don't exist. Either way, I needed to decide how to respond to all this.

I was about to turn and bolt when I tripped over a log. I tossed Candy out of the way as I crashed backward to the ground. I think a fern cushioned my fall. The fog covered my face briefly just before I was picked up and cradled in the male's arms.

CHAPTER 3

Darah

"Hey! Put me down!" Damn, he smells good. His hard-muscled body was sending warmth into me, soothing my pain away.

I wiggled, trying to get the big guy to let me stand.

"I need my backpack and guitar!" I was pointing toward my sleeping hole.

The male noticed my backpack and guitar case and grabbed my stuff. He placed me over his shoulder, and I slapped his ass and yelled.

"Put me down right now!" Blood was rushing to my head. I fought my combined desire and fear. I wasn't going to be handled by this neanderthal of a man. Tossing me over his shoulder like a sack of potatoes or something. It's just not dignified.

I focused on my gift, trying to get a sense of this guy's intentions.

I did not feel threatened by this guy, but being manhandled was just not okay.

I was swamped with the need to find safety. This feeling was not my need. It was coming from the purple male. My fear amplified; if this formidable-looking guy was scared, then I was terrified.

I saw Candy hopping alongside us, his pastel fur popping out of the fog with every jump. The male was hot, not just because he was all muscle and yummy, but warm, radiating heat. I couldn't resist his body heat and tried to warm my hands on his radiating hot back.

I heard him hiss at my cold hands. I felt his back muscles tense, but other than that, he kept his stride and moved fast. He was silent, stealthy. I was getting dizzy and needed to be on my feet.

"Hey! I need to be put down. I will faint soon if I cannot stand up!" The male kept on moving over the thick brush and ignored me. Candy locked his little eyes on mine. Did I see anger flash? I barely caught the glow of his fur before I lost sight of him. I tried to peek around this male's side.

I pinched him, "Hey, I said. Put. Me. Down!"

Candy jumped before him, his fur glowing, his tail waving at him like a weapon. The male suddenly stopped, jarring me. He set me down slowly.

I stood on shaky legs, and I had to lean on the male as my dizziness subsided. The male stood frozen with wide, dark eyes locked on Candy. I leaned down and picked up my glowing ball of fur. The male grunted; he looked fearful as he stared at Candy. I sense he fears Candy and doesn't want me to touch him.

"Don't be silly. A big guy like you is scared of such a tiny little fur ball." I said as I nuzzled Candy. His fur dimmed, and he purred. The male put his finger to his lips, indicating I should be quiet. He pointed up and then straight ahead and waved at me to follow.

The male occasionally picked me up and lifted me over more extensive patches of brush. Candy's fur lit up every time he touched me, and I had to coon and say, "It's okay,

Candy." What a sweetie pie! It was so protective of me. I was not scared of this male. Yet I was unsure of him. I didn't have many options at that moment. I would let him lead the way for now. I was just happy my little Candy was sticking with me.

Eventually, the dense tree line thinned out, and as we slowly made our way, I heard water, maybe a river. The male stopped, he was scanning the area and looking at the cloudy light purple skies. He pushed at my shoulders, urging me to sit under a giant fern plant to hide with him.

I wanted to ask him about the water. He put his hand over my mouth and then over his mouth. He shook his head. I guess he thinks we should be quiet. Candy approached me and rubbed his long ears and face against my thigh. The male glanced at Candy. He looked at me like I was holding a viper or something. My little fur ball hissed up at the purple man. I could feel the male's concern.

"What?' I shrugged as I rubbed my Candy's long ears.

We sat in the ferns, looking at the sky for a while. I was about to get up and go. Try to make my way to the water when the pretty light purple sky opened with a perfect circle, revealing the blackness of space and the twinkling stars. A pop sound hit my ears as a spaceship entered the sky from that hole.

It was black and looked like a huge battleship with wings. It hovered, lowering itself silently from the clouds. The male moved backward, making me follow him deeper into the trees. His fear turned terrified.

I had officially lost it. I felt like I was in the twilight zone. What the hell happened to me? And where the hell was I?

Spaceships and alien creatures. I was definitely not on Earth. I still wondered if I was in a coma, dead? Maybe . . . I didn't know how to wrap my mind around all this.

As it landed, I wanted to observe the spaceship, but the male tugged me, even when Candy glowed and hissed. For the first time, he showed no concern for my furry pal. His black eyes pleading with me as he grunted and tugged at my sweat-shirt. The male was terrified.

Something in my intuition said that if the male was this worried, I should be scared shitless. I mimicked the movements of the male and stayed low on the ground. I crawled behind the purple man. Getting a clear view of his ass and all his glory. Focus, Darah, I thought to myself that we were in danger , trying to calm my desire.

He crawled around a giant boulder, and the male tossed my bag and guitar into ferns. I almost squealed, my heart clenching as the bushes swallowed the sight of them. He motioned to a giant boulder lying up against a tree trunk. I followed and saw him squeeze into a break in the rock that hid the hollowed-out tree trunk.

I slipped right in, and we had to be cozy close inside the tree. Candy came in, too, not leaving my side. I adjusted myself to sit with my back against his chest. His hot body had me feeling snug and warm, the first real reprieve from my misery of this cold.

Assessing that I was in a tree with a horned male and a furry creature that glowed. While outside, there was a mean-looking alien ship that opened up the sky. Light purple sky and puffy clouds dispersed. Allowing a circle of night to form. Blackness with stars peeking through, framed by purple skies, casting a shadow over the ground below. I was mesmerized by the odd sight as the spaceship had landed not far from me.

I was so out of my element and still a bit shocked, as the warmth of the stranger behind me and Candy's softness oddly comforted me. I felt my exhaustion seep into me as my ears began humming. The sounds of movement outside had me stiffened as footfalls crunched leaves on the forest floor.

Radio communications in a language I could not understand echoed as the footsteps passed. I tried to breathe in and out slowly and silently. Eventually, all the noise went quiet again. We stayed in the tree for so long that I fell asleep.

A beautiful, ethereal woman appeared to me in my dreams.

I don't know her, but I recognize her, well, the feeling of her. I've felt her whenever I went to the botanical gardens in Austin. I had chosen that spot to spread my family's ashes because of the comfort I felt. Realizing now that this being before me was behind that feeling. My curiosity was burning up inside me, and I wanted to comprehend how all of this was connected.

"Darah, I have chosen you. I am the Goddess Harmony."

"My True mate, Hecat, is the God that created the planet Laverian and all its life there. I sent you to Laverian to help me save this world. My mate is arrogant and did not care for his creations properly. I intend to interfere and help his Laverian people. I need your help, my dear. Human women have helped me before. I believe in your perseverance and strength. I have come to favor you, human females. My mother has tied you to me and my world. She has tied you to Hecat's world as well. Therefore, you are my chosen one."

"The Laverian men have been targeted as slaves for the mining of moons and fighting entertainment. Due to their strength and primitive ways, they cannot fight the advanced technology of the neighboring planets. Most of life has been harvested from this world already. The Laverian females are taken as slaves and will suffer terribly as forced sex slaves. I am almost too late to save them. All the people and life of Laverian have been stolen and sold in the neighboring God Kane's universe and territory."

"I am still learning to communicate with you as you are in another realm. Time on the planets moves much faster than time in the realm of the Gods. So, I have to communicate back in the past from my perspective and the present from your perspective. My parents are strong gods, the strongest among us. They suppressed my powers to protect me. I am unable to communicate as I would wish with my ability muted. I sent you through a temporary God portal from Earth to Laverian and brought you here. I need you to . . ."The beautiful woman faded from my dreams as I woke up."

I woke startled and reached around in the dark. I felt horns with my hands resting above my head. I remember being in a small space in a tree with the big male. Pins and needles numbed my legs. I felt claustrophobic and needed to get out and get blood to flow back into my legs again. I wiggled my way out, waking up the male.

"Woman! Wait." The purple man growled at me. He grabbed my ankle and tried to pull me back inside the tree.

"Whoa, did you just speak English to me?" the male pulled my leg harder.

"Owe!" I kicked at him, and my leg started to get that painful feeling as the blood flowed into my leg again.

"Damnit, woman! Do you have any survival instincts?" The male hissed, trying to convince me to stay hidden in the tree.

"Don't talk to me about survival! Surviving is all I ever do!" I snapped as I awkwardly hopped around, trying to get through the pins and needles in my feet.

The male smoothly crawled out of the tree and scanned the area around us, taking a fighting stance. I realized I might not be safe, so I stopped hopping and sucked up the lingering pain. I looked around to see if the spaceship men were around.

My dream returned to me, and I realized I understood the purple guy. Was that dream a real encounter with a goddess? She said she would allow me to understand the universe's languages. That male only grunted at me before.

What was that Goddess's name? Harmony? Did she say Harmony? I was so confused. Did a Goddess kidnap me? Why? I think being in a coma was still a better theory. This must be a wild dream. Everything was so vivid and feels very real. If this was in my head, I must manifest things to start going my way. That's that.

"I need water," I said as I dug through the ferns, looking for my things. I grabbed my guitar and pack and started heading for the water. I made it to the clearing, where a spaceship hovered.

I rolled my eyes and said, "Fuck it!"

I started marching across the field and passing the spaceship to get to the tree line on the other side. I found a waterfall and a beautiful pond. I filled my pink water bottle. I usually boil the water that I collected in this way. However, I was in a coma, right? So, if this was all in my head, then I can theoretically control everything I saw. And dammit, I wanted to start making things happy and dreamy. I stripped off my dirty clothes, manifesting a warm swim in a summer pond. I dove off into the water.

"Fuck me, that sucks!" I came up with a gasp. The icy water stung my skin.

The demon man stared at me from the shoreline, a look of utter shock. My Candy was pacing back and forth, looking at me and then toward the spaceship. They look scared and worried. This was my dream, dammit, so they needed to get with the program.

"This water is fucking freezing!"

I stuttered as cold hit my bones. The demon looked at Candy.

"She is mad, insane!" The demon whispered angrily as he faced the forest, ready to fight.

Candy hissed in agreement, continuing to pace. I was so cold from jumping into the water. I rushed to get out. Stupid, I was hoping that all this was in my head and maybe I could manifest warm water in this pond.

I got out of the water and dressed. I put my soggy shoes back on as I heard men talking and walking in the woods toward us. The demon man grabbed me and silently whisked me off to hide behind trees.

For the first time, I saw the space people. They were four feet tall and thin in dark uniforms. I wanted to laugh. Skinny, short, tiny people. This giant male was scared of these little dudes.

Well, I assumed dudes they looked male to me. The men walked to the water, laughing at each other. Did all the spaceship guys come in pint-size? Apparently, my mind was a wild place. Candy sat stiffly at my toes, watching the spacemen.

What was I missing? The small man who held a little gray device in his hand pointed it at the water and pressed a button. A blue laser light hit the water, and a fish sphere was lifted from the pond. Hundreds of fish were stuck together in an invisible circle. The man turned with his buddy holding his device as the fish floated behind them as they walked back towards their ship. The guys never paid attention to the footprints I left or my bag on the shore. They seem intoxicated and giddy.

"So, they have some technology," I whispered, feeling a little disturbed by the amount of fish that came out of that pond.

"They wield the power only Gods could have." He explained.

"It is not the power of Gods. It is technology." I said, trying to explain.

"They have taken everything and everyone from my world. I would also be captured if I wasn't on my traditional excursion to bond with nature before I take my seat as chief of my village."

"My parents, my cousins, everyone I know was stolen. There is nothing left but the prill fish and us." The male waved his hand to include Candy and me.

Tears brimmed his eyes, and my heart flared in sadness for him.

"I am so sorry these space people took your family. I don't know how to explain it, but I need to get one of their devices. I think it will help us.

I started to follow the spacemen when the big guy grabbed me from behind to stop me.

"Woman, are you mad? Do not go after them."

My ears hum again, and I can sense the Goddess, my gut telling me to take one of the handheld devices.

"I need to grab one of their power things," I said.

"I am trying to keep you safe." He said, defeated, like he had no choice.

"My name is Terrek." He growled low and soft near my ear. "

Damn, this guy makes me tingle in the best ways.

"Terrek," I repeated to taste his name aloud.

I heard him moan when he heard me say his name. That sound alone is distracting in a delicious way.

"Yes, Terrek and we are bonded. I felt it the moment I saw you," he insisted.

"My duty and honor are to keep you safe and loved," Terrek said, his smoldering eyes locked onto mine.

"Keep me safe and loved?" Whoa, this was too much!

I go where you go. If you get me killed, so be it. We are bound,» Terrek explained.

"What kind of nonsense are you going on about?" I asked when he placed his hand on my mouth again.

He pulled me behind another tree as the two tiny guys ran past us, laughing and running into the woods. I licked at his annoying hand and was surprised at the sensation of butterflies that started fluttering. He removed his hand slowly. Candy was so still and close to my feet. I slowly made my way towards the hovering spaceship. Terrek was not amused. I felt his fear and frustration towards me.

Well, I was starting to think this all might actually be real. Either way, the next step is to get me a strange, remote thing. Maybe I can find a lightsaber mode. I grabbed my bag and looked back at my terrified boys.

"You coming?" I asked with a shoulder shrug and started walking toward the spaceship.

"I'll be damned. The spacemen are having a fish fry." I whispered as I watched the aliens preparing a cookout. There was a ramp that was extended to the ground from the ship. Little soldiers had an outdoor setup. I was not about to let us get stranded on this planet. I stepped towards the ship when

Terrek grabbed my hips and pulled me back further into the trees.

"Woman! They are small, but you underestimate them. They carry magic in their hands and wield power like little Gods."

"Fine, let's go after the two that took off into the woods."

I found the two men skinny dipping in the pond. How they could frolic in the freezing water was beyond me. I went to their stack of clothes, and I took as many gadgets as possible off the uniforms. The little men seemed intoxicated and enjoying each other's company. I got away with my haul quickly, but Terrek was very stressed. I took my stolen goods and laid them out before me as we hid behind a big tree.

"Let me see if this is the remote laser thing that grabbed the fish." I held it in my hands and read the buttons.

"This is too easy," I said with amazement.

The words were alien symbols, but somehow, I knew what was said. The blue button was a capture beam. The red button was kill eliminate beam. The green button was a disabled or unconscious beam. There was a reset switch and a fingerprint reader.

"See, Terrek, no magic here. You just need to be able to read the directions."

"Shit, my nerves are kicking in," I mumbled as I decided if I should hit the reset switch and placed my thumb on the reader.

I realized this was not an elaborate dream. I felt like this was all real. I was not on Earth; I was with an alien male and a furry creature. This planet was doomed, having been harvested. A Goddess had picked me of all people. How was this strange device supposed to help me, help us?

I heard that humming again, and my body just pressed the reset button. I could feel the Goddess's influence inside me, making me act.

My thumb felt a zap, and then the little remote went quiet.

Terrek jumped back, his black eyes terrified as I played with my new toy. I looked at him, His emotions swamping mine.

"It's okay, Terrek. I won't hurt you." He looked at me like I had grown another head.

"I don't want you to hurt yourself." He whispered, still very uncomfortable being out with the spacemen so close in the open.

"I need to understand these things to use them to protect us."

I put my remote weapon down and picked up a black wand thing. The side of the bar said the healer. The end had a reset switch and a button. I reset it to my thumb and pressed the button, waving it over my hand. I heard Terrek hiss as I waved the beeping wand over my hand. I saw a white light scan my hand, and a pulse began. I felt a warm tingle as my hand healed from the thorn that had bitten me. Terrek sank to his knees in wonderment.

"You can wield the power of the Gods?" He asked.

I did not have it in me to be dismissive of his feelings. I reached out to touch his cheek gently.

"Oh, Terrek, honey, this is not God's Power. This is just technology."

Terrek leaned into my palm. I felt his affection toward me. His need for my comforting touch. I found myself attracted to this raw side of Terrek. I wanted to comfort him. His grief and pain are a reflection of my own. Shaking that off, I tried to explain.

"I can read the instructions on the device, and it seems easy enough."

I showed him the remote weapon and explained the buttons. And showed him the wand.

See, it›s a tool, like your net or your bow and quiver.»

"I know what tools are, woman. I just haven't ever seen a tool like this."

I picked up another gadget, and I read it as well. It said mass stasis sleep containment. I wondered what that was?

There was a device the size of a cell phone that said Captain Requirements Educator.

It all conveniently had the reset feature. The humming in my head was starting to irritate me. I needed to reset it and add my thumb to this device. An urgency that was taking my own will away.

"Okay, already!" I snap at the air. Terrek gave me a shocked expression.

"Sorry, Terrek, but I have to reset this one too." "I need to," I said as I pressed my thumb to the small scanning area. I had an instant information overload that started streaming into my head. I couldn't quite understand the sensation. Suddenly, my head eased up, and blackness took over.

CHAPTER 4

Terrek

My heart stopped when my crazy bond mate fell over as if she had died. She had been trying to convince me these God powers were harmless tools. I am failing at being her bond mate. Reluctantly, carefully, I placed that device in her bag with the others.

That Infant Chetaht was hissing angrily at me as I pulled my bond mate over my shoulder to find a safe spot to hide from the Kanenites who invaded my world.

This foreign woman was fascinating and infuriating all at once. The Kanenites have gathered and stolen most of my world's people and animals. I was the last of my tribe, the last of any life left on my planet, along with the Chetaht and my alien mate.

I wondered how she had traveled to my world, but my guilt was all-consuming. What kind of Chief will I be for my people? I guessed I would never be chief now. The Laverian people are now somewhere up in the stars.

The female that I found myself bonded to had fainted after

she touched her tool. I had to carry her to this cave. She had been asleep, and I was worried she wouldn›t wake up. I Heard the frantic rhythm of my heart pounding, like a wild beast trapped in a cage trying to escape. My ears pounded and added to my desperation. I needed my mate safe and unharmed.

The night sky was so beautiful I often took smoke next to an open fire just to gaze up and wonder what lived beyond the stars. Now, my heart clenches because anger will always fill me at the sight of the night sky.

Life exists up out in the stars. Evil had come and stolen my people. I was on my traditional excursion where I dressed as our ancestors would have, and I lived in the wild for thirty rotations to become one with the land that provides.

This was the way of my kind. My father is retiring as Chief, and he wants me to take on the role of Chief since it is my time to lead. I was three days from being complete with my thirty days of wild. when I saw the signals from my village when the invasion happened. The sky lit up, and these flying ships swooped down and attacked.

By the time I made my way to my home, my village was vacant. The spacemen stole everything from me. Everyone I knew was now gone. My parents, my people.

I was nearly captured by the tiny ships that scanned my land when I discovered that this cave hid me from the God power of the space machines.

These spacemen have scanners to find us. I saw them use the scanning thing that flew around when they took the animals. In a matter of days, they have taken every living thing. I had tracked this baby Chetaht after I witnessed the creature's pride captured days ago. I don't know how this little one was over-looked, but when it bravely left its den early to seek out its mother. I knew I had to capture it and ride out what was left of our life together. Either that tiny beast would devour me, or the spacemen would capture me.

I felt nothing but guilt and loneliness. The man I was reduced to, became a hopeless soul. I was weak and at a loss.

I had contemplated ending my life. I am a Laverian warrior male, the next in line to be Chief. I am supposed to be stronger than that.

I am supposed to honor my people in all my actions. Their fate utterly haunted me. I have no idea what these Kanenites are doing to my tribe up in the stars. I had decided to focus on saving that abandoned Chetaht kit, I made that my priority. After all, he was left alone like I was.

These Chetaht's are vicious, even at the size of a kit, so I was reluctant to grab it. I fashioned a net to catch the tiny beast. When I finally saw the kit again. I swooped it up in my net only to be confronted by a feisty fearless alien woman.

She came out of nowhere to rescue the creature I was trying to save. To my shock, the woman lit a flame in my soul and initiated my mate bond. She is unlike any other female I have ever encountered. She lacks horns and purple skin, however I found her enthralling still. She is so enticing and beautiful that even the Chetaht kit attached itself to her. I have never heard of a Chetaht being tamed, not even a kit.

Chetaht's are the apex predator in my world. They gave the Kanenites hell, trying to collect them. That freezing blue beam was the only way they could collect these wild beasts.

I was wallowing in my doom. My tribe was stolen, and my planet was wiped out of all its living creatures. I just wanted to try to save the kit. Now I have my mate. My soul wanted to celebrate, but I was distraught because I was doomed to watch her suffer, maybe even witness the spacemen take her too.

I figured in a few weeks, when this kit grows to its full size. I would end up being the Chetaht's last meal. It is better to go out like that than face the fate of being alone and starved to death. Now I have a bond mate who seems insane and doesn't care about her safety. I don't know how to save her. I thought I'd probably die soon trying to save her.

Looking at all the iron cores peeking through the rock ceiling, all I was feeling was my soul was grieving for the life we should have had together. Suffering for my people, what fate do they face? I was so angry. I wish I could fight and save them. I was powerless against the God power the spacemen wield. Why had the God's forsaken me and my world? I was being tormented.

I was almost convinced that God's powers were just advanced tools until she hurt herself by touching the God's power. I picked her up and ran off to take her to safety, with a Chetaht hissing at my heels. I want to know the name of this beguiling female. I vow to realize it before my demise. I have a stack of smoked prill fish; it is not good, but it is part of the diet I am to have when I am on my traditional excursion. I had offered the growing Chetaht beast a stack, and it hissed at me.

"What, not good enough?"

That creature curled up next to my sleeping mate. I longed to do the same. I wasn't going to fight that little beast to do it. Besides, my mate was not ready for me to hold her. I wondered if I would ever get the chance.

"Fine, I need to sneak off to catch fresh prill. When my mate wakes up, she will be hungry. "I had snapped at the beast.

Prill fish was the only food available, and I hoped the spacemen had not found my secret water hole.

"Keep her safe while I am out getting fresh fish," I muttered in defeat.

That infant beast chuffs at me. I left the safety of the cave. I piled a bushel of branches over the entry so it would stay hidden from view. Most of the ships had gone. Two flying machines have been making rounds with their scanners, looking for resources. I figured the ship that landed in the open meadow was the last.

My planet was doomed. If we could evade capture, we would eventually starve. Being hidden in the cave has kept that scanner from detecting us. I suspect the metal veins in this cavern have somehow shielded me. I am unsure if being captured would be a better fate.

I made my way to the water hole, and it was small. I have been placing prill fish in it to stalk pile a food source. I pulled my catch box up, and a pile of prill fish flapped. I assumed that was about the last of my fish. My stomach clenched as I thought of my beautiful, creamy-skinned, blue-eyed alien woman. Her long, dark blonde hair looked so silky I wanted to run my fingers through her hair so badly. My heart rushed like the rapid rivers near my home. Keeping my hands to myself was hard. She was back at the cavern, and I wanted to hurry. I did not want her to wake up alone.

Fighting my need to mate her and seal our bond was all I wanted to do now that I had recognized her as my true bond mate. Circumstances were not ideal. I was ashamed that I could not give my mate what she deserved. I wondered if these aliens brought her here. Maybe she had escaped somehow. However, she seemed like the sight of them was new to her. I had so many questions.

I don›t know how she got here. I had never seen her kind before. I recognized her as my bond mate the moment I saw her. So, I cared not where she came from. All those mate responses I had only heard about until then had me feeling wrapped up in desires and urges to complete our bond. Both elation and bitter sadness wage war in my heart.

This insanc exotic female seemed scared of nothing and was remarkable and infuriating all at once. All I wantcd was to keep her safe, loved, and happy. My heart ached with failure, and I didn't see how I could spare her misery. The life I had imagined when I discovered my bond mate had been stolen from me by the spacemen.

I had no good future to promise my female. It was too dangerous to take her to my home. The attacks had damaged my village, but my home still stood. Out of my reach, too dangerous to return to. I searched for survivors and barely got away before the scanning flying machine could find me.

I made my way back to the hidden cave. My heartbeat was fast as my eyes settled on my sleeping mate. Her beauty had me captivated. Gods, I needed to know her name. She laid peacefully down on my pallet of furs. I wouldn't say I like bringing her here—a dirty, primitive cave.

I had prepared a pot of prill fish stew for my mate and me. I had offered a pile of fresh prill for the growing beast.

"You like your meat raw," I said as I sat beside the fire, holding back my urge to hold my mate.

I was disgusted that my only option was to offer her prill fish. I need to try to get my female to drink. She had slept for two rotations. If we die here, I can only hope our next life will give us a happier experience together. She deserved better, the best kind of life.

I had only dreamed of being mated and giving my mate all of my love and protection. Building a family and making memories of a happy life together. My dreams shattered, and I was facing a catastrophic short life ahead with my new mate. I had cried out, cursing the Gods for such a fate.

The stench of prill fish filled the cavern as I tried to give water to my sleeping mate. I sucked in a trembling breath to calm myself because I was a failure to my people, and now I had failed my new bride while she was sleeping. I needed to be stronger than that for her.

Would she ever wake up? I wondered with a deep sadness.

I really needed to know her name. Before death came to steal away my future, if nothing else, I needed her name. I would search for her in my afterlife. If I could speak her name before I died.

"Please drink, please wake up my bond mate." I had spoken.

CHAPTER 5

Darah

I felt water pouring into my mouth.

"Drink, female!" Terrek pleaded in a soft, deep tone. I sat up, spitting out a mouthful of water.

"Woah, what the hell!" I choked out.

Being waterboarded awake was a shock. I opened my eyes and felt my head zap with dizziness. It took me a minute to focus on my vision. We were in a cave, and it was dark, lit only by a small fire. I was sitting on a bed made of furs. I saw Terrek kneeling before me, waving my pink water bottle at me.

"Give me a minute." I had held up my hand to stop him from pestering me.

"Thank the Gods, I was worried if you did not get substances, you would perish." The man was concerned.

Confused, I sat up and looked around.

"What is that awful smell?" I mumbled as I saw Candy chowing down on a pile of fish.

"Well, butter my butt and call me a biscuit!" I said, shocked that he looked twice the size he was the last time I saw my fur baby friend.

Candy stopped eating when he noticed me. Candy happily bounced up to me, knocking me back down on my fur bed. He started to purr and licked my face enthusiastically.

"Ewe, fish breath. Yeah, yeah, I love you too." I giggled.

I had pushed the medium dog-sized cotton candy ball off me. I was patting him on his head, his fur not as puffy anymore. I began petting his big rabbit-like ears. He was transforming into a predator-looking beast. I was beginning to see why Terrek would be scared of Candy. Not me, though. I felt nothing but a sense of family and affection from Candy.

"Go finish your dinner. Gross." I had encouraged as I wiped Candy's drool off my cheek.

"How long was I asleep for?" I asked, feeling dazed by Candy being so big.

"What is your name, female?"

Terrek asked, shoving my water bottle at me. I grabbed the water and took a long swig of it. I was looking at Terrek staring at me with his sexy black eyes.

I wiped my mouth and smiled.

"Darah Davis, it's nice to meet you, Terrek." I reached out my right hand to shake Terrek's hand.

He gently placed his giant hand on mine. He held onto my hand longer than a handshake required and said.

"Darah Davis." In a low, sexy purr that made my whole body react to him. His nostrils flared, and hunger bled into his black eyes.

I wanted to kiss his lips to see how it would feel. When suddenly, hunger pains cramped my gut, and all I could think about was food.

How long was I asleep?» I groaned.

"Two rotations," Terrek said with concern.

Here, eat this.» He handed me a wooden bowl of fishy soup.

"Thanks." I took the bowl so hungry I didn't care that it looked and smelled disgusting.

I drank the soup, trying not to gag. I held my nose shut, hoping it would help, but it didn't.

"I am sorry, but that was disgusting," I complained. Terrek laughed.

"I know, however, Prill fish is the only meat source available on the planet. The Kanenites have harvested all our sustainability."

Tears brimmed his eyes. He cleared his throat to continue.

"I am sorry you became my bond mate when death is upon us. I can offer you no future here. You, me, and the Chetaht will die in weeks.

"Terrek, my sad demon, it will be okay, you'll see." Can I have some hot water, please?" Terrek looked confused as cute wrinkles furrowed his brows.

"Darah, you realize I am not this demon male you speak of. I am your destined bond, mate.

I rubbed my ears. Maybe my understanding of universal languages was off because Terrek had just declared I was now his wife. Bond mate means soulmate. It would equal marriage on Earth.

"Do you not have bond mates in your world? I have never known anyone who does not know of bond mates. Their soul's bond when mates meet for the first time in a destined everlasting bond. Usually, a bonding is celebrated quickly. The need to mate and seal our souls together is strong, and the consummation of being bond mates creates a love that can never be severed." Terrek explained with pleading dark eyes.

He stiffly poured hot water into a clay cup and handed it to me. I felt a vibe of hurt and jealous emotions rolling off of him.

"Look, Terrek, I like you. I don't understand the destined mate bond. But if you want to date, I will consider it. I am attracted to you. I don't think I am much of a partner for anyone. My family died. I am no longer on my home planet. I haven't had a moment to deal with this since I arrived here." I dug through my pack, looking for my tea as I rambled. Adrenaline was pounding in my heart.

My confusing emotions swirled. My body and soul were wrapped in a wave of happiness when Terrek said I was his bond mate. I needed to embrace him and kiss him all over. I also had a logical reaction that told me there was no way I would marry this guy at first sight. I don't even know him.

"I understand now that I am no longer on Earth, my home. My head cannot come up with this on its own. Between a Goddess humming in my ears and the spaceship. Those devices downloaded everything that I needed to know about commanding a spacecraft. Well, call me convinced. I am no longer on Earth."

I poured my tea into my cup of hot water. Terrek just watched me, fascinated.

"You are a sexy horned man, Terrek, unlike any male I have ever known. Earthlings don't have horns and purple skin on Earth, my home planet. I am just trying to make sense of everything so strange to me." I said.

My grief over my family settled into the forefront of my heart again. I prayed that Terrek would understand my need to take all this slow.

"I am not a boyfriend. I am your bond mate. I am loyal to you. And unless we have other destine mates, it is you and I from here on out." Terrek said matter of fact.

I took a sip of my tea and watched Terrek. He was serious about this.

"On Earth, people meet and get to know one another. If there is mutual attraction, they date. If things go well, they might marry and have a family. Sometimes, it goes wrong, and they get divorced. We don't have fated mates. Some people claim they are soul mates, but I don't believe in soul mates." I drank more tea as I assessed Terrek and his reaction.

"Go wrong and get divorced. What does this mean?" Terrek asked.

"You know, separate and find other people to love instead."

I read my leaves at the bottom of my mug, stars, nothing but stars again.

"Bond mates cannot separate and love any other that is not a destined bond mate. How can Earth people be certain of their future and family if they do this divorce thing? How can they deny the gods will? Before birth, we have a chosen fated mate to share our souls with our bond mates. It is the core of our life to discover our love." Terrek was baffled by my Earth custom.

"We will work out our communication skills later. Other destined mates? I am not sure I understand you and this bond mate's business. Let's shelf this discussion for later. Right now, we need to steal a ship and save ourselves." I said as I packed up my bag.

"Can I keep this mug? I asked as I placed it in my pack, wrapped in my dirty clothes. I secured it in the grocery bag and tucked it in my backpack.

The humming in my ears made me want to move faster. Time was running out.

"No! Darah! We are not going near the Kanenites. I will not have you harmed or taken. It is too dangerous. We will die, and I just got you. At least let us live out what time we have left without making me watch you get stolen from me." Terrek was adamant.

"I've been through way too much shit to starve and die on a strange planet." I snapped.

I grabbed my guitar and left the cave with my Candy at my side and a broody Terrek following.

"I decided I would get myself together and make my family proud. I owe them that. I will live my best life for their sake. So, we will steal that ship and figure out how to find a way to live. I wasn't educated by that device to sit here and starve." Terrek insisted on carrying my pack and guitar.

Terrek looked proud. He stood tall and bowed his head in respect for me.

"Spoken like a true Laverian, we will die fighting." He said proudly.

"I will follow you, Darah, my mate.

Terrek insisted on carrying me again, "Darah, it will be faster, and I can be stealthy if you allow me to carry you."

"I can keep pace. I don't need you to caveman carry me." I started to move, not giving him a chance to argue.

Candy stalked close by, stealthy and silent. I didn't think I would travel so quietly. I heard every crunch echo loudly and cringed as Terrek raised his brow with a look that said I told you so.

"I will fight by your side, my Darah if we live through it. I will show you how to move silently through the woods. I will teach you all I know."

I smiled at the big man, my fear kicking in the closer we got to the spaceship. The incessant humming in my ear drove me to do this. Rationally, this is just reckless.

It was turning dark, and the Kanenites gathered in rows of attention in front of the open docking ramp.

"They do this before they are about to leave the planet," Terrek whispered.

I reached into my bag and grabbed the device that the educator taught me would sedate them in masses as a way of capturing slaves without resistance. I turned the device on and walked up behind the tiny men.

"Howdy, guys!" I said as an introduction.

I tried to zap the lot of them. But I messed up because the stasis beam, I needed did not engage.

"Shit!" That was not good!

The aliens were stunned momentarily by my presence, and then chaos broke out as they rushed at me. Candy pounced on the closest male to me. These guys moved like ninjas.

Candy quickly tore through two of them. Terrek was in the fray as they swarmed him. He was tossing them and breaking a few like they were twigs. I heard the cracking of bones and the cries of pain from the Kanenites as Terrek and Candy brutally fought back, trying to keep me between them. The copper smell coming from the dark blue blood of the spacemen had my stomach churned. A few aliens exited the ramp, pulling their devices off their hips.

Time to get this right. I had taken my device up and watched my finger hit the stasis button.

This time, they all fell into stasis, floating in invisible bubbles. Damn, that felt satisfying. I walked past them and went up the ramp. Terrek and Candy followed me.

"Darah, I am glad you used the tool before these Kanenites. I thought we would be zapped and stolen for sure," Terrek said with relief.

He looked at Candy with respect instead of fear.

"Good boy, for keeping our Darah safe." Terrek praised.

He spoke with admiration as we walked into our first spaceship together. A hallway that was white and lit up and greeted us. My backpack and guitar case seemed unscathed, hanging off Terrek's back. I sighed, grateful and surprised after that violent fight.

I followed the hallway and passed the doors that looked like an elevator. The humming in my ear led me to head straight for the one at the end of the hall. There was a keypad. I entered the sequence code that was educated into my mind, The door slid open.

I walked into the command station of the craft. Three spacemen looked at us with wide eyes. Terrek roared and attacked, taking out the two men that charged me. My fur ball pounced on the third spaceman and brutally ripped open that guy's neck. I swallowed bile at the sight of the blue blood. My sweet fur ball can pack a punch.

"Gross!" I said as I went to examine the control panel.

I reset the whole system to recognize myself as commander. This was the most exciting thing I have ever done and the most overwhelmingly violent thing. My stomach was still rolling over the gore of it all.

I scanned the craft for lifeforms and saw prill fish and life pods in the storage cargo area. Spacemen in a sleeping quarter were scheduled for the next shift. The rest of the spacemen had been outside for final formation and count before taking off. I sent a wake-up call with orders for them to report to cargo for a stasis failure response.

I sealed the handful of men into the cargo and placed them in a stasis hold using the ship's AI security droids. I had them secured with the other spacemen that I had collected outside. Then, I moved them into a holding storage compartment. This was similar to playing a video game.

I secured all doors and sealed us in for space travel. I hovered our new spacecraft over the pond with the waterfall and remotely sent the prill fish back into the pond from which they had been stolen. I took us up, out into space, and turned on the view monitor to see the magnificent display of Laverian and its ringed moons.

Terrek dropped to his knees and watched in wonderment. This was the coolest thing I ever did. Candy hissed and cowered in a corner. I was blown away. I managed to steal and fly this spaceship. The craft tried to auto-pilot and fly us to a pre-determined course. I used my new knowledge to override the command.

I hovered outside the atmosphere of the planet Laverian. This moment felt magical. I looked at Terrek, and he was feeling it, too. Candy quickly adjusted and seemed to calm down. I examined the panel readings, learned about this ship's layout, and reworked the system. I cloaked my ship from outsiders. I saw logs indicating the location of a port for the slavery trade. I took note. That had to be important. Maybe we could rescue Terrek's tribe.

CHAPTER 6

Darah

I saw plans for the harvesting of the Laverian planet and plans to assimilate the resources of the next planet on their list, Gias. I decided it was time to teach my big guy, Terrek, about technology. I waved to the educator in front of Terrek, who backed away from me."

"Terrek don't' be a baby. I promise it will be fine, and you will thank me later."

I tried convincing him that he needed to use the educators. Candy hissed at Terrek when he moaned with annoyance.

"My mate, you ask me to wield the Kanenites tool. It is dangerous." I grabbed his hand, intertwining our fingers. This feels nice holding his hand. I liked the contrast between his purple skin and mine. His hands felt strong. "Focus, Darah," I silently chided.

"Follow me. I want to show you something. I held his hand as he and Candy reluctantly walked with me to the chow hall. I went to an alien machine and requested meals for Terrek, Candy, and me."

"Here, Terrek let the machine scan you, stand here." I watched as Terrek reluctantly stood where I pointed.

"I do not like the scanning machine." Terrek was apprehensive.

"I know that it scans your mind, and the AI can simulate your food requirements. If you have a specific dish, the food dispenser will replicate that dish. This is as close to mindreading as I can imagine," I said in awe.

Terrek allowed the scan, and then Candy sat for me like a good boy while he was scanned. I stood to get my scan. Once the machine processed us, it began to run.

To my delight, the food dispenser made me steak and mashed potatoes. It was slightly off with texture, not quite the real thing, but close enough. Terrek had a Laverian dish, candy, had some raw meat.

We got drinks, the Chetaht got a big bowl of water, I had sweet tea, and Terrek had Laverian punch. I felt blessed and amazed that I could manage the operation of these machines so well.

"I am full as a tick!" I said after we all ate our meals. "My momma always said big decisions are best discussed around the kitchen table." Food has a way of making everyone feel better about hard things.

"You say the oddest things my little earthling." Terrek said with laughter.

"Terrek, it's just technology." I said with the last mouth full of yummy sweet tea.

"Please! How can I convince you to get educated by the machine." I practically begged.

I saw his face light up.

"I will let you use your tools on me if you grant me one kiss, Darah. I don't want that thing to fry my brain before I get to taste your lips."

All of a sudden, I was hungry in a whole different way. I got up from my seat and crooked my finger at the big guy, beckoning him to me. The sight of that man, with his hypnotic black eyes, zeroed in on me.

I looked up as he towered over me, pushing me back against the wall. I reached up and pulled his ram-like horns down, bringing his lips to mine for a searing kiss.

He moaned with a sexy growl, lifting my ass so he could stand, not breaking our kiss. Whatever Laverian food he ate added spice to my lips as I got lost in his taste. I ground into him. My need was like a burning building.

I broke our searing kiss. "What was that? "I panted as I locked eyes with his."

"Our mating bond will only become stronger, the need to mate." He said.

I could smell Terrek's scent of pine and male and felt something intense happening between us.

"Darah," Terrek said in a soft plea of need.

I pressed up to kiss him again, he had an amazing mouth. His kiss was thorough, deep, and lingering. He was taking his time to explore me.

I felt this need for him more than lust, magical of some kind. We genuinely were connecting soul-deep.

My clothes a barricr, I tore myself away from his lips.

"Put me down, Terrek. I need to take these clothes off."

Dazed, Terrek held me to him as I wiggled out of my sweatshirt and let it fall to the floor. My skin came alive as we touched bare chest to bare skin.

More than that, we began to glow. An iridescent light sparkled everywhere our skin touched,

Electrical currents spark across our skin, white lighting connecting us."

"What is this? I caressed my hands across his chest and felt the delicious tingles the electric light stimulated inside me."

"This is our consummation. The mate bond is binding our souls," Terrek says as he peppers kisses that spark across my chin.

I kissed him again as his muscled chest melted to my soft

breast. He purred as he laid me down on the cold table. He helped me take my jeans off. I watched him as he pulled away the layers between us.

He dropped his leather cover with a pull of a string, and his fully engorged cock stood hard and intimidating with his girth and length.

Naked, I reached for his dark purple cock. I went for him. He hissed out in pleasure as I grabbed his length and mapped out his cock with my hand.

Lubrication was secreted from his tip and allowed me to massage him easily. I want to taste him so badly that I bent down over his cock to take him as deep as I could in my mouth.

"You're killing me." Terrek moaned, holding my head.

He tasted like sex and the flavor was all his. I needed to have him fully and claim him. I felt this instinctive need to be his, to make him mine. I laid back on a table and displayed myself in a way I never had before.

The power I felt as he looked at me like I was precious and all his. I was full of need, and this moment was life-changing. Terrek went to his knees and took my core into his mouth.

He moaned this sexy growl of delight as he ate me and all my juices. He focused on my clit and worked me until I went over the edge in the best orgasm of my life. He climbed on top of me and kissed me passionately, mingling my flavor into our kiss."

He growled low and sexy, holding his cock at my folds, rubbing back and forth, waiting to enter me.

"Oh! God! Yes, Terrek, yes!"

I arched up for him to fill me. Terrek moved slowly, stretching me deliciously full. He slowly seated himself fully into me. I kissed him, begging him to move faster as he allowed my body to adjust to his size.

He moved to make a pace that had my orgasm exploding again. This time, I was clamping down and gripping him tightly. I had this undeniable urge to bite his shoulder, so I did, drawing blood. Claiming him, I yelled.

"Mine!" As my orgasm ebbed.

He roared, "Mine!" As he spilled his seed.

He held my face in his loving hands and kissed me with his coppery blue blood on my mouth. I stayed in the bliss of it until he broke our kiss and helped me up. Seeing the blood drip down off his shoulder had my senses return, and I felt instant guilt for hurting him.

"I am so sorry I hurt you." I tried to use a napkin from the table to hold to his wound and stop the bleeding."

"You gave me your mate mark. It is how we complete our mate bond." Terrek looked so proud as he showed me my bitemarks."

"I don't want to hurt you. I feel bad." Terrek kissed me tenderly.

"Never feel bad for this. You did not hurt me. You honor me, my love." Terrek kissed me again, and I felt how genuine he was.

I just wanted to stay with him and feel the magic between us. We were still in the chow hall. Now that I got my bearings, I picked up our clothes and shoes and had Terrek follow me to the captain's quarters, where Candy was already sleeping. I showered with him, and we lay naked in the soft bed, talking."

"This bed feels so amazing, Terrek. I have been sleeping outside for six months. I forgot how amazing a bed could feel."

I stretched out in pure joy in the aftermath of our lovemaking and reveled in the unbelievable new reality I found myself in.

"Let me explain my home and my family to you."

"I want to know everything about you, my Darah."

"Tell me about your family?" Terrek asked as he moved my hair off my cheeks. The gesture was so sweet and caring."

"I lost my mom, dad, and little brother about six months ago, haven't felt whole, haven't felt anything but grief until I ended up here. Being with you feels unreal. Feels like magic. I feel guilty to be happy in this moment, and I am also grateful I can feel anything other than the nightmare of grief."

I softly explained through tears.

"Darah, I hate that you have lost your family. I suffer loss, too. I dared not have hope until you came along, and now I hope to one day see my people, my family, again. I am proud to have you as a part of that." Terrek Kissed the top of my head and pulled me close to him.

"The world I knew was simple and solid. Now, I fly among the stars with my alien bride, who has the favor of the Gods. All the doubt and heartbreak of my world being stolen from me somehow seems to melt away when I am with you, Darah. I will fight by your side and follow you to unknown worlds. You are my hope. You are now my home. I hope that I can be that for you as well. I hope together we can rescue my people." Terrek said.

I spent the night sharing my life story with Terrek. He was just so sweet, genuinely holding me as I cried, recalling my family and that accident that took my whole world away."

"I am so sorry your tribe did not gather in support to aid you during your time of grief," Terrek said softly, kissing my forehead.

Terrek had difficulty grasping the idea that Earth had so many inhabitants, yet there were homeless people and hungry suffering alone."

"You are too sweet, Terrek, but in my world, it is a fend-for-yourself place. My family was my little tribe. They would have moved mountains for me if they could. When I lost them, I was just lost."

"My tribe has our mates and our family units, but we all support the village." Terrek said.

"If a child was orphaned, the neighbor will take the child if there is no other family. If an adult were to suffer a loss as you did. The adult gets adopted into the neighbor's family. No one should grieve alone. Everyone craves family. I don't know of the tribes of Earth, but our people unite."

"We are the guardians of the land, keeping the wild pre-served, monitoring our land. Being mindful of her health. We work hard and celebrate with merriment as a tribe. We are stronger together and will fight to protect our kind. However, we never stood a chance against the Kanenites God's power. We never expected evil from the sky."

"I lost my tribe and my life in my world. I am so sad that I cannot share that with you now. How beautiful life with my tribe could have been."

I leaned in to kiss my man, heartbroken for his planet and everything he had suffered.

"Terrek, I am so sorry you have suffered. We both lost so much. I am here with you now, and we will figure out how to get past all this pain. I am unsure how either of us ended up here. Together, we will figure out the next step."

I fell asleep in a soft, warm bed, clean and full. My arms and legs wrapped up around this strong male. I felt a sense of peace for the first time since my family died. I drifted to sleep and had another vision of the Goddess Harmony.

–Darah–

"Darah, sweetie, I am glad you are adjusting so well to your true mate, Terrek. He is a good male," The ethereal Goddess Harmony said in a voice that sounded like a song."

"Thank you for blessing me and sending me on this amazing adventure," I said, not understanding why a Goddess would ever pick me for anything."

"My dear Darah, I am afraid I have a big job for you. My mate Hecat has made a whole universe of creations. However, Hecat has left them unattended and vulnerable. Laverian is such a beautiful creation. "

"The God Kane had his creations mettle with worlds that are not his to mess with. So much is not fair and out of balance. I am the Goddess of Harmony and balance, so my parents named me Harmony.

I will not allow this to continue. I am with Hecat in the realm of the Gods. I will aid you to help right the wrong of Kane's meddling." The Goddess looked very concerned.

"I don't think I can help very much. I am a mess. I lost my family, and now I am out in space with an alien male whose whole world got invaded. How can I be any help?" I said, wondering what the Goddess could possibly need from me.

"Do not underestimate yourself, my dear Earth female. Just follow your intuition and do what feels right." The Goddess smiled sweetly at me.

"You need to move now. To find the people of Gias, of my Hecat universe, and make an army to stand with you against the Kanenites." The Goddess Harmony faded as I awoke.

"Wait! What about my family? Can you check on them in heaven?" I asked as she started to fade. I mean, she is a Goddess, right? I did not know there were gods and Goddess's but I thought my family went to heaven, I mean I hoped like any of us would.

Now that a Goddess has sent me off into outer space, I just wanted to check on my family. I mean, can my family look out for me in the Hecat universe? So many questions. I woke up with an urgency to find Gias.

"Did you have a bad dream?" Terrek asked me as he hugged me closer and kissed the top of my head.

"Oh, hi, good morning, big guy," I said as I detangled my limbs from Terrek."

"No, not a bad dream. I saw a Goddess in my dream, and she asked me to help her help your people. I am a bit over-whelmed. I wanted to check on my family to see if that is even possible. I don't understand everything that is happening to me." I said as I tried to wake up.

I saw hope flicker across Terrek's face, and my stomach dropped. I didn't know how to help him, but I would try for him.

"I am not sure I can manage much, but if I can help your planet and people, I will do whatever I can," I promised.

I went to the clothing dispenser device. It scanned me, and I picked my options and dressed in a simple black outfit. Then, I helped Terrek get an outfit, too.

I opened my door and went to the dining hall, where Candy was pacing back and forth, waiting for breakfast. Candy was now the size of a grown cheetah on Earth. He made an aggra-vated chuff sound, letting me know he was hungry.

"Okay, big boy, I will get you a big hunk of meat," I reas-sured him, and he rubbed his head on my thigh with a purr.

I fed us breakfast and introduced coffee to Terrek. The mind reading simulation coffee was almost perfect, but it was a bit bitterer than I recall coffee tasting. Terrek seemed to enjoy it.

"Um. That was like my rising root brew of Laverian. It wakens and energizes." Terrek said, excited for coffee.

I made my tea and saw warrior women in the leaves. My

intuition told me that Gias was our next stop. I have a feeling these women will be very intimidating warriors."

"Well. Are you ready for the educator?" I asked as I brought out the educator devices to teach Terrek. I found a cabinet of them. This all feels eerily easy, its been my experience, the other shoe is about to drop when things fall into place to easily.

Maybe these Gia's females will end up being trouble. Or maybe not, but the trouble was on its way. I will take these devices, which will give me an edge, even if it's a small one. Terrek needs to be just as informed. I hoped that I had convinced him thoroughly with our lovemaking.

"Yes, anything for my mate. You did grant me that kiss, after all." Terrek said.

I sensed his trepidation about the God's power. He was trying to hide his fear for my sake.

Terrek submitted to the device and fell asleep to assimilate all the new information uploaded into his brain. These artificial intelligence devices fused with the brain, allowing information to be inserted and extracted. If we truly wanted, we could be cloned and assimilated with an avatar or cyborg.

My mind can't wrap around the science of it or the morality of it. Every time I use these devices, does that leave DNA? Does it leave my essence that can be cloned? I will try to forget that tidbit and pray that no one wants to create more of me.

I am off to greet Gias and try to make friends, as The Goddess Harmony requested. She has an indescribable way to influence me and my direction.

CHAPTER 7

Darah

I took out my guitar and sang my favorite songs as we flew. Candy laid his big, fluffy body at my feet. His fur was no longer bright pastel; it was still colorful but more subtle. I sat on the captain's chair, flying to the planet Gias.

I was strumming my song, really getting into the music; as Terrek slept, I reflected on all of this. I was still grieving, but I was ready to try to pick myself up and be someone my family would be proud of.

Being sent through a god portal and thrust into this wild situation. Terrek's raw grief over losing everyone and everything has my own grief swelling. I need to be strong to get through this. I want to be able to help Terrek so he doesn't have to face all this alone.

I know how heavy alone feels while grieving. If a Goddess picked me for whatever reason, then I'll be damned if I don't do whatever is necessary to try to make things right for Terrek and his planet. There is hope, and as long as the people of his world breathe, then there has to be a way to save them.

Otherwise, what good am I? I'd have never had a god on my side before. So now I wanted to make things right for Terrek. That would make my family proud and spare Terrek even more grief. The music fades as my hands stilled when an alarm beeped on the display dash, indicating a life pod opening in the cargo area. Terrek was still asleep, adapting to all the knowledge downloaded into his brain. I looked at Candy, who became on alert, sensing my concern.

"Come on, boy! let's go check it out." I put my wand on stun mode and approached the cargo.

My thumbprint opened the sliding doors. These Artificial intelligence systems can scan the bio of any living thing. If the program is reset, then it's easy to access. Having the Goddess bless me with the ability to understand the language of the stars. It made reading Kanenites writings a win for me because the instructions were too easy. I guess they don't need much security if they don't count on non-Kanenites to be unable to translate their language.

There is something so thrilling about having control of this ship. I stepped into the cargo area. Cubicle units held the cargo loads in by an invisible electric wall. A slight shimmering was the only view of the electric field that contained and separated the cargo.

I saw that the AI cargo machines and droids had put all the spacemen in bubbles still in stasis, packed securely in a cube containment unit. The machines scanned Candy and me and then returned to their spot in the ceiling. Candy hissed and paced back and forth.

I continued walking past the cargo units toward the cargo that was setting off the alarm. I saw a wall of pods. Adult body-sized life pods made of dark-tinted glass. One was lowered to the floor and opened.

A beautiful human-looking female lay in her pod, slowly waking up as the AI mechanical arms and scanners moved all around, checking her vitals and waking her up.

My heart sank, feeling scared that another human was

trapped here by the enemy. I rushed to the pod, and a machine scanned me, giving me the green light because I was the ship's registered captain.

The woman was dark-complected with long black hair. She opened her dark brown eyes, and her groggy, sleepy face slowly became aware. The white fabric that molded her in her body released its hold and retreated into the pod›s side, exposing her nakedness. She was long and lean, and she had glamorizing beauty.

Candy hissed and growled, pushing at my legs to move back. The sleepy woman sat up slowly, shaking her head. I stepped back and rubbed Candy's ears, trying to calm him. The woman finally noticed us.

She gasped in fear at the sight of Candy. Candy snapped his fangs at her, hissing as he put himself in front of me. He aimed his tail at her, reminding me of a scorpion about to strike. Candy's coat started to glow.

"It's okay, boy. We don't know if she is a friend or foe yet." I tried to move around him to greet the female.

To sense her and see if my gift could detect anything. I was cautious and even more uneasy now that Candy is highly agitated by this beguiling female. Her beauty feels off, dangerous.

An image of an orchid mantis flashes to the forefront of my mind. Candy hisses and growls. Reminding me that some petals can eat you. I step back and straighten my spine. I will not show this female any fear.

Candy roared at the woman, letting his fur glow bright and bending low, ready to pounce, while his tail was prepared to sting like a scorpion. The woman looked terrified. She gasped in fear, tears brimming her eyes. She brought her hands to her mouth. She looked scared, but something is not right. Somehow, I don't feel like her display of fear is real.

"Please don't let your beast eat me!" She pleaded with soft whimpers.

My ear picked up an echo between her authentic dialect and my understanding of her translation in English. She used her hands to brush her hair behind her ears nervously—her un-human-like ears. They were pointed and drooped a bit, reminding me of the pig's ears on the ranch back home. Her ears were more feminine and dainty on her, though.

"My name is Darah. Who are you, and how did you get here?" I asked.

I was grateful my tone was even and didn't give away my inner nerves. Maybe I should have tried to wake Terrek before coming here to investigate that alarm.

My heart squeezed when she flinched like I was scaring her. But something in my gut was alarming me as well. My intuition is not giving me a solid read. Maybe it was just Candy's reaction to her. He doesn't like her. The bottom line is that she seems wrong.

The woman started to hyperventilate, clearly terrified and exposed. Tears poured down her face. I felt bad now. She was so upset and scared. But Candy stood his ground and looked ready to pounce on his prey.

My instinct was to comfort her. I know waking up in a strange place with aliens was scary. I have to be mindful of the underlying feeling that was nagging me. This woman was dangerous.

"Please, I beg you, don't let it eat me." The woman cried, terrified.

My heart sank seeing her so scared. I felt like this was not my genuine reaction, though, almost like I was being influenced. I wonder if this alien is using some trick on my senses.

I reached for Candy, rubbing his ears. I walked before him. He growled and looked wicked and mean. I stared into his eyes, getting him to focus on me instead. He hisses, not liking me interfering. He buts me with his head to get me to move.

"No! Candy, Stop!" I said very firmly. "I know, she's lower than a snake's belly in a wagon wheel rut, but we can't chop her head off just yet." I whispered into his big ears.

He looked at me with hurt eyes. It reminded me of a dog that got in trouble.

"That's a good boy," I said in my fur baby voice.

If she is the bad guy, I promise I'll let you eat her,» I said loudly as I looked at the female, giving her a warning.

I just petted him as he chuffed and reluctantly moved to my side.

I stood tall and looked at this woman.

"You're safe, for now," I told the lady as a robot arm laid a jumpsuit next to the woman.

She grabbed the outfit without looking at Candy, who sat beside me, chuffing and glaring at the woman.

"My name is Andromeda." She said meekly.

The woman got dressed and stood in front of me. She was tall, maybe five foot ten. I rubbed my ear, trying to get used to the echo and the odd translation. Her lips moved and seemed out of sync with her words. It was strange. I wanted to compose myself as I faced her.

"I'd say it's nice to meet you, Andromeda, but I don't know you yet." I tried to look confident as I spoke to her. She needed to be aware that I was in charge.

Candy hissed as if to say, "Yeah, what she said."

I rubbed his ears as he rubbed up against my thigh. The woman looked at Candy and me like we had three heads. She placed her hands up in the air.

"I don't know how I got here. I was taken from my home. I walked into my home, and someone grabbed me from behind. I heard two males talking, and the next thing I recall is waking up here."

Andromeda looked scared and seemed very vulnerable. I wanted to believe her, but that feeling was not my own. Candy's hackles raised as he started to glow. The woman tried to step back when the pod stopped her from moving further.

"It's okay, Candy," I said, and he calmed down, letting his light dim to his normal pastel fur.

"I suggest you stay a few feet from us until I decide it is safe for you."

"Gladly." The woman said as she stared at me.

I looked at Candy, taken aback at how his face turned menacing when he looked at Andromeda.

"I imagine you're hungry, so why don't we start there? Follow me, please."

I turned and walked to the chow hall as Candy walked behind me. He kept his tail pointed at the lady like a gun. Odd, I will have to ask Terrek about the Chetaht breed and see what that was about.

CHAPTER 8

Darah

I sat at a table as I watched the woman get her food. She sat at another table and faced me as she ate. I petted Candy as he still pointed his tail at her and stayed in front of me. I noticed he kept himself between Andromeda and I at all times.

"What planet are you from? Who are your people?" I asked, trying to get information to research and learn about this female. She looked scared, and I felt a bit bad for her. Again, I could tell it was not my genuine response.

"I am from a small planet called Tarin. It is more of a moon world as we are a satellite to a giant gas planet in the terrain sector. I need to look up that planet. I haven't had much time to figure out many things. While trying to get to Gias, I hope the planet Gias will hear me out. I needed to find time to look up this Tarin planet at some point soon.

"I heard whoever had grabbed me say to his companion that he liked how I looked for a class three planet. For an inhabitant from the Terrain sector." Andromeda shrugged.

"I never knew space people existed. I am sorry I ever found out." The female pouted.

I felt a sense of her lying. Maybe she was just scared, and I perceived it as some kind of manipulation of my senses.

I am sorry the space people kidnapped you. I did not take you. I just took this ship to save myself and my people. Lucky for you, I was successful.»

Her eyebrow rose curiously as she looked at me. Candy tensed and started to glow. His tail still pointed at her.

Calm, boy, it›s okay.» I soothed as his fur dimmed again.

"Can you just take me home, please?" The woman asked tearfully.

I went to a thumb screen and activated the wall tablet. I scanned the charted stars for a route to Tarin. It was in a system far from Gias. I really needed to go to Gias first.

"I'll Tell you what, I will take you home, eventually. But you need to wait. My crew and I must make a stop at Gias. We have a job to do, and I can't ignore it. Lives are at stake. If you are trustworthy, I will take you home. If you lie to me, betray us, I will let Candy eat you, we clear?" I stared her down.

Andromeda was tearing up, her lip trembling as she looked at me, scared. "Yes, I understand."

Something in my gut has me alarmed. So, I would keep one eye open concerning her. My empathic ability seems blocked when reading her energy. That in itself was unnerving. I scanned her thumb and locked her out of my ship's systems, only allowing her access to a room I assigned her and the chow hall.

Andromeda looked relieved when I left her in her room. Candy relaxed fully as the doors slid shut. His tail was swooping without that stinger point.

I went to check on Terrek sleeping. The sight of him calmed my frazzled nerves. I snuggled with him, letting all my unease fade. Feeling safe next to Terrek, I slept for the night. On day two of Terrek's sleeping, I took Candy to the chow hall and fed him his meat. His portion doubled with his growth.

In a matter of days, he grew so fast. He was somewhere between a leopard-size and a horse now—a giant cat-rabbit with his hop and prancing movement. I opened a room next to ours so Candy could have his own bed. I made sure his doors stayed open. I would never have imagined the little baby fur ball becoming this big predator. I am glad he loves me.

I opened the doors to the crew showers, and Candy used a space in the corner for his potty spot. The clean bots took care of the cleanup. I liked this captain gig so far. We should arrive at the planet Gias in the next cycle of this ship's timer.

So, I am guessing that means tomorrow. I expect Terrek to wake up soon, probably hungry and disoriented. My monitors show that the Tarin woman has not even left her room to get food. I walked to her cabin to escort her to the chow hall to ensure Andromeda ate.

Candy was even more fierce-looking now that he was so grown. As we approached her room, Candy started to glow, his tail on stinger mode, facing her door.

"No wonder she won't even come out to eat. She was terrified she would be the one eaten," I said to Candy, petting his head and his big rabbit ears.

"Now stop being so mean, Candy. Let her give us a reason for it first." I scolded him.

He let his fur dim but kept his tail trigger up and pointed. His face was still menacing as I opened Andie's door.

Knock, knock. It's me, Darah. I just wanted to make sure you get something to eat.» I said, waiting outside the door in the hall.

Andromeda slowly stepped out into the hall with us, her wide eyes on Candy's tail. She stepped farther away from us, keeping several feet back.

"Yes, I am hungry, thank you," she said sheepishly.

"I told you before. You are welcome to eat whenever you want to. I gave you access."

She hurried to the food dispensary. She got her food and

drink and sat two tables away this time and watched Candy and me wearily.

"Why didn't you come here to eat?" I asked curiously.

"Your . . . uh . . . pet won't let me leave my room." Andromeda jumped a bit when Candy started to glow.

"Candy!" I chided with my fur baby voice.

Let the lady get some food.» I looked at her and shrugged.

"He is a bit protective."

Candy started chuffing as Terrek walked into the chow hall.

Andromeda stiffened as Terrek came into view.

"You woke up a bit earlier than I expected," I said and went to kiss him, happy to see him. His tender gaze hardened when he noticed Andromeda at the table.

"Who is this?" he asked, stepping before me.

Great! Now, I have two beasts overreacting and putting themselves in front of me. I maneuvered myself to stand next to Terrek and grabbed his hand.

"Terrek, Babe, This Is Andromeda from the planet Tarin. I looked at her. This is Terrek, my mate and partner."

Candy growled, pacing in front of us, his tail pointed at the Tarin female.

"Settle down, Candy," I said as he sat reluctantly beside my thigh. Terrek relaxed as I held his hand.

"Nice to meet you. Please call Me Andromeda. I am not your enemy."

My inside turned hot with a tinge of anger. Somehow, I felt like this was a lie.

"Hello," Andromeda," Terrek said softly as she looked up at my huge Laverian male.

"Now that introductions are out of the way, I need a moment to chat with Terrek."

"Candy, keep an eye on Andromeda for a few minutes, don't eat her yet," I ordered.

Candy hissed as if to disagree, licking his fangs and pointing his tail towards her as I took Terrek's hand and stepped out into the hall.

Andromeda attempted a smile that did not reach her eyes.

"I won't give you any reason to hurt me. I want to go home." She said.

Her terrified and sad disposition felt like a forced glamor.

"Terrek, I don't trust that woman. Something is off with her. We must be mindful of that." Terrek looked at me, his black eyes drawing me in.

"I already know she is not to be trusted, my sweet mate Darah. I felt like she was trying to mesmerize me like the ground serpents do when they focus on their prey. They sway and seem docile, like a loose branch that swings in the breeze, luring the rodent to its doom. On my planet, it is a secretion of scent that causes the tiny brain of its prey to feel safe and long for connection with the serpent. While it gets into striking range, where there's no escape.

This female is no meek little thing, we shall not underestimate her, maybe we should put her in stasis along with those Kanenites."

"On earth, we say keep your friends close, but keep your enemies closer." I looked up at Terrek.

"I want to watch her and see what we can learn. We can pretend to be friendly to a point. She will need to show us who she is and what she wants at some point. We agree, then, we will be careful not to trust this woman?" I had asked.

"I don't understand. Why keep your enemy closer than your trusted friends? I disagree. Any threat to you, known or unknown, needs to be eliminated. I think she should go into stasis. Why risk it? We both feel she is bad."

"I gave her access to her room and the dining area. Candy has the room next door to us, and he has his door open. He will keep her in her place. I think her fear of him is truly genuine. I have just started experiencing aliens and space beings. I want to learn as much as possible, even if it is scary."

"Darah, I don't like this, but you were right about the educator. I have so many questions, and I want to learn so much more. In this matter I will let you decide, however, if she tries to hurt you, I will eliminate her on the spot."

I laughed, "You may have to get in line, I promised Candy, I would let him eat her if she turns out to be the bad guy."

"You may regret that. Chetaht's eating their prey is a brutal, bloody mess." He said with amusement.

"Gross." I shook off the unwanted image in my head.

"How's your head?" I asked, moving a thatch of hair behind his ear before I cupped his cheek in the palm of my hands. He groaned in a pleasant way and rubbed his face into my hand.

"My head hurts slightly, but it was all worth it to have learned so much." Terrek pulled me into his hard, muscled body that seemed to mold me into him.

"Damn, you smell so good. I love how you hug me." I peppered kisses on his chest as he kissed my head. I loved that simple show of affection from him.

The door behind us slid open as Andromeda step out with a mean Candy pacing back in forth behind her like he was herding her, he even snapped at her feet, making her jump.

"I am returning to my room now. Please keep him away from me," Andromeda begged.

"Sorry, I have to let him watch you, or he may get out of control, obsessed with you, and decide to eat you without permission. As long as you are the friend you claim to be, you should have no worries. Candy has to watch you to see for himself." I said as her door closed.

I put an AI viewing monitor to follow Andromeda around the ship. She was only allowed to access the areas of the ship I gave her access to. But having her monitored at all times helped my nerves. I had the main viewing screen open as we saw the stars blur by outside. As we approached the planet Gias, a class six in the star system, we were in cloaked form.

I looked up Planet Classes after Andromeda mentioned it when she overheard her captives. Class three is a low-tech primitive planet, with no contact allowed from class four and above alien species. Earth would be a class three planet. A wild preserve protected by galactic laws. So, this Tarin female would not know space aliens or culture any more than I would.

Class four to class seven are under the galactic law of the Hecat universe, or so the Kanenites spy's special report said. They were able to chart out a course for Gias based on the captive they caught and tortured for information. Gias was the next planet on their list to harvest.

I don't know much about the ranking other than the higher the number, the more technologically advanced the planet. I can only hope the advanced beings of Gias will be accepting of Terrek and I. Hopefully, they would appreciate our warning them of the impending attack.

"My mind is full of the God's knowledge. I can work on these devices now. Woman, you have gifted me an amazing blessing." Terrek thanked me with a quick kiss as he scanned the ship's security system.

I loved that he could distract his grief by focusing on learning this craft with me. He was so full of hope to be able to save his people.

Laverian was a class two planet, considerably low-tech, and protected by the wild preserve of Galactic law. For these Kanenites, to invade and harvest resources from Laverian was an act of war. I will use this information to ask for help saving the Laverian planet and rescuing its inhabitants.

A message rang to my ship's AI asking for an access code to permit entry beyond the planet's protective barrier shield. Alarms blared as we were targeted by satellite space fighters set up for planetary defense.

"Shit just got real!" I said to Terrek.

Feeling scared, I lowered all my defense systems and opened coms to receive communications. I took a deep breath and stood tall and confident, praying no one could see past that façade. This was all pretty far out for me, too. Fake it till you make it was my new motto.

Somehow, I knew the Goddess blessed me so that I could adapt and accept all this new alien stuff. The ability to read and understand was fantastic. Translation was part of my soul now. I needed to realize that not everyone was so blessed.

I found the strength in Terrek. He was so attractive and calm amid so much new information. His whole idea of the world had expanded, and he was adjusting stoically. I love this guy. I just do.

CHAPTER 9

Terrek

Unease had me stand up and move to Darah's side as the ship was hailed by the planet Gias. I trust Darah and her plan, but I cannot bear to lose her now; everyone at this point was a danger in my mind. Whatever we face, it will be together.

"I am Darah of Earth. I come in peace. I come as an ambassador of the Goddess Harmony."

She stood tall in front of the camera monitor, allowing Gias to see her as she greeted them. She left the ship unshielded, unarmed, and utterly open to attack. A stunningly beautiful woman with red eyes appeared on the viewing screen. Stern-looking and serious. Something inside my gut stirred.

"Fuck!" I said in an exhaled whisper. That red-eye-female was our mate bond. I recognized her.

"You will follow our escort ships to port, and we will greet you at the dock. If you arm your weapons, we will eliminate you." The red-eyed female warned.

Darah just smiled. "Understood. See you at the dock."

Darah glanced at me, silently questioning my "Fuck!" remark.

I just shook his head and mouthed, "Later."

"Okay, buddy, you got some explaining to do later," she said.

The Gias red-eyed female had no horns, her dark red hair was pulled back in a tight knot on her head, I craved to see her hair fall loose. I wanted to see more of her but viewing screen only showed her face and the dark collar of her uniform. Her alluring face highlighted her bright red eyes. The Gods saw fit to pair me with two gorgeous pale skinned aliens.

Darah flew her stolen ship as we followed the two mean-looking crafts that flew next to us, the viewing screen showing us the angles and storing the information on the systems of the ship. As the AI examined the crafts, I watched with curiosity. I thought this ship was terrifying with its scanning and the God's powers.

The escort craft has weapon's that moved on every part of the surface that faced us a show of force. This had me worried. The Gia's battleships were intense and intimidating.

The blackness of the craft was so dark it faded in and out of view. As one flew circles around us, scanning our craft, the weapons retreated to the surface and came out whenever the craft changed positions as it scanned. The craft seemed huge on the viewing screen.

The two intimidating ships escorted us through the laser weapons grid surrounding the planet. We saw a docking station hovering like a satellite above the planet's atmosphere. Darah landed like an expert in the space station bay.

We left Candy to guard Andromeda's door as Darah and I exited our craft to greet the soldiers waiting on the dock. A line of battle-ready figures cloaked in head-to-foot-black military gear stood as a show of force to greet us. I raised my empty hands, following Darah's movements.

The vacuum of space sat peacefully behind us. The interior was metallic and the ships and droids seemed organized. The air was crisp and clean, but the grouping of warriors had me on alert.

Hello, I come in peace,» Darah said in greeting.

She smiled a friendly smile. I moved in front of her and growled a warning. They don›t seem too friendly to me.

"It's okay, Terrek let me by." She insisted as she took steps to stand next to me.

I reluctantly allowed her to stand tall next to me. It's not the best position for me to defend her. I just wanted my Darah to be happy.

A tall female moved through the small army of beings before us. They parted a path as she came forward to meet us. This is the lady that was on the monitor. Our mate. Her eyes scanned my mate and then ,they roamed over me assessing us.

Her stern face flickered with a slight look of recognition and shock. Our new mate understood that she was our fated mate. I gave her a knowing smile. Our new mate recovered quickly and regained her warrior stare. When her eyes met Darah's again, she spoke.

"Why have you come?" She asked firmly.

"Hello, I am Darah of Earth, from another universe far away. This is my mate Terrek of Laverian. We have come because I was asked to by the Goddess Harmony. I want to show you something." Darah said.

Darah offered her a tablet with the logged information.

"This has information that shows how the Kanenites have been harvesting and selling slaves taken from class two and three planets that go unnoticed. Also, you will see that Gias is on the scheduled next to be harvest. You will be attacked soon. We came to warn you and ask for your assistance to help us rescue the people of Laverian." Darah explained as she handed it over.

A vast machine started to scan our ship that was parked behind us. The invisible atmosphere shield protected us from the space outside the port.

That would have been mesmerizing if I wasn't so worried for Darah's safety.

"I go where Darah goes." I demanded.

I hoped our new mate was a worthy soul. All these devices made me uneasy. These Gias soldiers were not friendly.

"Come." The red-eyed female with dark red braided hair demanded as she turned and walked to a door on the dock. I couldn't help but admire her ass as she walked ahead of us. I could not let this female distract me. I struggled to ignore my need to embrace this new female.

Darah and I followed the lady to the door. A scanning laser washed over Darah and I and beeped green. We were allowed to enter through the door, and we continued to follow the tall, fiercely sexy lady. She ushered us into a small waiting area. We sat in black chairs while two armed guards watched us.

"Stay here until I return." The woman simply said.

She looked me up and down and then scanned her eyes over Darah. She momentarily lost her stern expression again and hunger bled into her eyes. She seemed to catch herself and quickly resumed her hard disposition as she turned and left us to wait without another word.

"She seems cool like a cucumber," Darah said as she rolled her eyes.

"I am not sure I expected such a cold greeting. Plus, I have a strange urge to follow that female. Is she another alien that secretes pheromones to lure prey in?" Darah asked quietly to me.

"I don't trust this place," I said with a growl eyeing the two guards.

"As far as that woman, no Darah, that is not a deceptive feeling. She will be important to us, Darah. I will wait calmly with you and see how this turns out," I said softly so only she could hear.

"Is this about that "Fuck!" comment earlier?" she asked.

"Yes, later will be a better time for an explanation." I said as I noticed the soldiers and the scanning machines watching us and our every action.

"Okay."

"The Goddess Harmony sent me here, so I was going to trust that. I wonder what you sensed about the red-eyed female that would make you feel she would be significant. Important how?" Darah asked.

"I need you to trust me, too. I will speak to you about that privately." My gaze fell on the two guards. I looked at all the scanning lenses that targeted us and the guards as my silent plea for her to realize we were not having a private moment.

"Oh, I see." Darah whispered to me.

"I can't believe they have us sitting here just waiting," Darah said with a pout.

"I am here with you." I pulled her hand to my mouth and gave her a gentle kiss.

We both relaxed a bit as we waited. Darah almost dozed off on my shoulder when the red-eyed female returned.

"Hello, Darah. I see you have found some troubling acts of treason that we need to address." The Gias female announced.

I looked at my new bond mate, wondering when she would reveal herself to us with acknowledgment of our bond.

Darah sensed something too, I could smell her arousal and saw the hunger in eyes as she gazed at the red-eyed beauty. I don't think Earthlings have the same sensations of recognition when meeting a fated mate as we do. What would be the best way to approach this situation? I know it is rare for my people to have more than one bond mate. But it is known to happen occasionally.

I never imagined myself with this luck. Harmony, her Goddess, indeed blessed Darah. I will defend and love her wherever she goes. If this sexy, Gias's female is as fierce as she seems , Darah will be very protected indeed. I needed to provide and protect both these fascinating women.

"We are on the outer atmosphere docking port, a heavily guarded entry point before you can get to the surface. We will take you both to the transport pod now so we can travel down to the planet's surface." Our new bond mate explained.

This ship was an oval shape, not nearly as intimidating as the escort fighter ships were. This craft was seamless and smooth. The shiny black surface opened and a ramp laid out before us. My mind was trying to understand what I was seeing.

"How can the surface move with no hinges or seams?" I had asked.

"We have the most elaborate updated technology and resources available to build the best defense system the universe has to offer." Our new mate stated as we settled in our transport seats. Her voice ebbed in my ears like a velvet purr.

"May I ask your name?" Darah asked interrupting our future mate before she was able to explain more. The two guards came in and strapped themselves to the wall in front of us.

"We are going to the planet to our council hall. You will be interrogated and determined worthy or not." The female flatly said as she buckled herself and stared in front of her, not looking our way.

"I guess not." Darah said, as she looked at me with a spark of anger in her eyes.

"On Gias and in general the galaxtic empires require everyone to prove worthiness before we welcome them. This is common knowledge. Since the two of you do not seem to know this yet. I will explain only that much, even though it is not usually done. If you are deemed worthy only then will I speak with you freely." Our mate said in a whisper with her sexy eyes locked on the wall behind us.

"I am eager to stand worthy," I said confidently.

The woman's brow raised. She was intrigued by us as she tried to stay stern.

"Is this why you refuse to tell us your name? Darah asked.

"When you are deemed worthy, I will tell you, my name." She said softly.

Darah shrugged, "Well, okay then." She said as we landed.

My chest tightened eagerly, I needed to learn the name of this female too. I held Darah's hand as we made the quick walk to get to the council hall.

A huge, tall building stood before us I had to look all the way up in order to glimpse the light reddish sky. The building was white with the smooth surface like the craft. It seemed like it was made of one solid seamless glass, a dark glass that was not reflective.

"It's hotter than Satan's hell cat." Darah said as she pulled against her collar and pulled her arm sleaves up when we exited the craft.

We were escorted into the building as the seamless glass opened allowing us entry only to become solid the moment, we all were inside. The floor was smooth and grey. I could not tell if it was stone or some alien element unknown to me. The walls were grand with a design that was framing many weapons.

"Yes, it is much cooler inside here." Darah said with relief. I reached out to take her hand.

There was a viewing screen that had a show of many different flying crafts that flashed one by one showing off its armor and weapons. We followed our warrior woman down a bright hall that had many more weapons on display.

She opened a door and took us past many open seats. At the front of this large open room, she asked us to sit in these big chairs that sat in display before a raised seating area.

I looked at Darah, her brave face fell briefly and I saw the fear she tried to hide. She made eye contact and I tried to tell her without words how proud I was of her and I was here whatever we face. We were locked down in place. I growled in protest, my nature wanting to resist the bindings.

"We will be fine." Darah tried to soothe me.

I am feeling a bit claustrophobic myself.» She softly took a deep breath.

I did not like her discomfort, but I knew she wanted me to

play nice for now. I certainly did not want to fight when first meeting our new mate.

We were facing a raised panel. A group of females walked in and took seats. By my count, twelve females sat staring down at us. The red-eyed female that brought us here stood off by the wall next to the armed guards.

The leader was older, intimidating, and gorgeous all at the same time, her red hair highlighted with gray, her red eyes piercing and missing nothing in her hard evaluating gaze. She took the center seat and spoke directly in front of us.

Test the newcomers now.» She demanded as machines came out of our chairs and probed us. A suction of some kind was applied to my forehead, and everything went dark.

CHAPTER 10

Darah

The Goddess Harmony came to my mind in my dream. Or I felt like it was a dream.

"Darah is worthy, and so is her mate."

I heard her chiming with her magical melodic voice. Her mate, Hecat, stood beside her. I heard the collective gasp of the audience that surrounded us. Murmurs of our God and Goddess appearing before us.

"This is the Goddess Harmony. She is my true bond mate. You will obey her as you would me." Hecat declared pridefully.

The images of the Gods before us were overwhelmingly powerful. Somehow, I knew that this was just a projection of them. The scrambling of movement was all I heard, with subtle cries and whispers of reverie.

"We praise you, our God Hecat." "We welcome your Goddess. We praise her, as well."

Harmony turned to me. Stand Darah, you are worthy. She smiled at me so beautifully that it hurt to look upon her. The straps of the worthiness detection chair flew away from me with a flip of the Goddess's hand.

Harmony gave me a warm feeling. She covered me in love and affection as she faded from my dream. I awoke standing tall with all of my five-foot-two frame.

My eyes scanned the stunned faces that surrounded me as they rose from the prone positions they took while going to the floor in submission to the Gods.

"Wait, that really happened?" I said out loud.

In a haze of shock, I numbly turned to my mate, who was still in his chair. The worthy chair that held Terrek displayed holographic images above his head.

This shows Terrek as he discovered his village and his despair for his people. I saw the beautiful structures that made up the homes in his village. Earthy style homes reminding me of cabins. My heart broke for him. I wanted to remove him from the chair when it glowed green, deeming Terrek worthy.

I ran to him, ignoring my chair, which had been flashing green since Harmony released me from the machine. Terrek stood fast from his chair. He shook his head, seemingly confused. I grabbed his hand and stood silently as we faced the council women.

The females were bowed with their heads on the floor, up on the panel in front of us. I was confused as I looked around. The red-eyed female and the two-armed guards also bowed on the floor.

"Uhm . . . is everything okay?" I asked softly as my voice echoed off the walls of the hall. Terrek looked at me wide-eyed.

"As long as I have you, I am well." He spoke sweetly.

Terrek was looking into my eyes with wonderment. "Aren't you just a tall glass of sweet tea." I winked at him.

The red-eyed female rose from her reverie first as the two gods faded from our view. She quickly joined Terrek and me, assessing us with a spark in her gaze. There was a softness in the lady with red eyes as she helped Terrek and me sit beside her. We watched all present shake off the wonderment and power of the god's visit.

The stern woman from before was gone as she looked us both over. It was enthralling to have her attention. Her changing disposition from cold and aloof to alluring with interest had my stomach flutter with butterflies. Before I could even evaluate my reaction. My focus was drawn to the booming voice of the leader.

"There was no denying the feeling of the Goddess or the feel of our maker, the God Hecat." Announced the woman in charge with graying hair.

Reverently, she turned her head towards the ceiling as if saying a silent prayer. She slowly regained her composure, standing to re-seat herself before the rest of the room followed her example.

"Welcome, Darah, the chosen one of the Goddess Harmony."

Every female placed their right fist over their heart and bowed toward me with a respectful salute. I mimic their greeting, bending back at them.

"Thank you for finding us worthy," I said.

"You have graced us with the blessing of the gods. How can we assist you.?" The lead woman asked.

"I need your assistance fighting for my mate's home planet. We need to fight the Kanenites and recover the resources that were stolen. According to the ship's files, the Laverian people have been sold for slavery. They were only a class two protected planet. I read the Spies report and have learned this much. I read they intend to harvest Gias next. I am hoping my enemy being your enemy will compel you to assist us, we need to save the slaves and resources that these evil beings have harvested. Please, will you help save the Laverian people?"

"We know of some things based on that tablet you gave us. I do not know how this planet was left undefended, but I will find out. We will need full access to your ship to gather as much intel as possible for our new quest. Our duty and honor to rally with you and fight these Kanenites."

"Thank you," I said in genuine gratitude. Terrek pulled me in for a hug and held my hand.

"My mate, ready to fight for my tribe and planet, Darah, I love you." He gave me a sweet kiss.

I had almost forgotten that we had an audience when I heard the red-eyed female clear her throat to interrupt us.

I felt my cheeks blush as I turned to face the council again.

"Sorry," I said as I stood tall, composing myself. Terrek squeezed my hand reassuringly.

"I am Empress Zion. We have much to discuss. However, it may be wiser to show you to our guest residence and let you relax for the day. We can resume our discussions tomorrow." The Empress said as she nodded toward us and turned to leave, dismissing everyone.

"Wait! I can't stay here. I need to return to my ship. I have Candy and Andromeda on board."

The Empress stopped and looked at the red-eyed female next to Terrek and I. "Escort her to her ship and assist her with whatever she needs."

"As you wish, Empress Zion." The red-eyed female bowed her head respectfully as the council of females as they left us in the hall.

"Empress Zion. Sounds important." I whispered to Terrek.

"Yes, she is the most important among us." The female who now gives me butterflies said as she and the two guards approached us.

"My name is Flame. I am glad you are worthy." Flame bowed with her fist placed over her heart, greeting me officially.

She was as pretty as a peach and her new disposition had me wanting to know her. Wanting to be close to her.

"It is very nice to meet you, Flame." I said, mimicking her, with my fist over my heart as I bowed.

Flames sultry eyes met mine, and something stirred inside me again. She gave me a smirk that said she knew something

I did not. Flame broke her hypnotizing eye contact with me and gave Terrek her full attention. I felt him jolt as my hand held his.

I get it. There is something about Flame. A fitting name for her as she ignites my insides with need. I saw them stare at each other as if no one else existed. Should I have been disturbed? I felt a sense of joy, a feeling of compersion, witnessing some intimate bonding between my mate and Flame.

I wondered if Flame had that effect on everyone. She had just gazed at me like that; I was still trying to shake off the warm tingles she had given me. Maybe aliens just had that effect on beings.

"Come now, tell me about Candy and Andromeda as I take you back to your stolen vessel." Flame had spoken as she broke eye contact with Terrek and tried to compose herself.

Terrek looked at everything with bright, dark eyes. He had a boyish charm about his curiosity as we followed Flame.

I told Flame how the Goddess sent me to Laverian and how I met Candy and Terrek. I caught her up to how I ended up there on Gias and how simple it seemed to take the ship from the Kanenites. Flame paid close attention to me as I spoke.

Her gaze felt tangible whenever she looked upon me. I was eager to keep her attention now that her coldness was gone. Flame seemed scary and formidable at first, but I'd quickly forgotten. I only had a desire for her, and everything I saw was remarkable and alluring.

"I want to have our technicians scan your ship and learn about the Kanenites' ability to fight us." Flame said suddenly, professionally.

She glanced at me and then Terrek, and before our eyes, she shook off her soft allure and became all business. The contrast was a shock. I tried not to let my hurt feelings show as I opened my ship's doors, lowering the ramp so we could enter my stolen ship.

"I know they used translator chips on the slaves. They store them in the infirmary so the slavers can give commands. But I understand that it is a limited translation. If needed, I can translate anything on board if that helps." I announce, trying to be helpful hoping to get her soft intoxicating attention again.

Flame called for her technicians, she took a scanning device, and they followed us on board.

"Gias has AI translation tags throughout our planet and ships. It scans the mind and feeds the natural speech into our tags so we can speak freely to visitors. The Laverian and Earth languages is now known to the Galactic Empires." Flame said. My mind blown from the wild advancement of the AI scans.

"The Kanenites must have a less advanced translation system than our Galactic empire source." Flame mentioned with intrigue.

We found Candy, his pastel colors glowing with his tale pointed at Andromeda in the chow hall. I walked up to him and started to rub his ears.

"Candy, are you harassing Andromeda again?"

He just chuffed and let his fur dim as he rubbed against my thigh. He gave Terrek a look. He's still not his biggest fan, but I could tell Terrek was in a better standing than Andromeda as far as Candy was concerned.

Candy saw several of the Gias people as they entered the room. He gazed at them and stepped in front of me, never taking his pointed tail off our life pod guest, who was now to his back. My sweet Candy doesn't like her.

"I would keep your distance from my baby Candy. He can be a bit moody at times," I warned Flame.

She seemed impressed by my pastel-colored guardian. She waved the group of her soldiers to step back a few feet.

"That's an understatement," Andromeda said with attitude.

"Hey now! He hasn't eaten you yet." I said playfully as I pulled on his big ears.

"This is Andromeda. I found her in the cargo life pod area. I also have those Kanenites spacemen in stasis down there too."

Flame was harsh towards Andromeda as she assessed her directly. Flame's stance and menacing gaze toward Andromeda looked like she was about to fight Andromeda herself.

"She needs to be deemed worthy or not," Flame said with a wicked grin, daring Andromeda not to be worthy. This woman was sexy and scary all at once.

"What does it mean to you and your people to be worthy?" I asked, curious.

"Worthy means you are good. Not worthy means you are bad. We won't give our positive energy to evil things. We fight bad, unworthy beings. We don't want evil to grow and infect our universe. Worthiness is essential to establish right away." Flame said as she glared at Andromeda.

"Okay, I think I understand that. But Andromeda claims she is from a class three planet. I am from a class three planet as well. We don't have machines that scan people to tell us if people are worthy or good or bad or evil. I was raised to give people the benefit of the doubt. Which means trust someone until they give you a reason not to trust them."

Flame looked appalled at that notion. "You trust unknown people before knowing they are worthy? Evil beings cause harm." Flame said.

Candy smelled Flame's outreached hand and seemed to accept her. He allowed her to step closer to me. We sat a table away from Andromeda as his tail aimed her way, ever vigilant.

"You see, even your beast scans for worthiness." Flame said as she sat next to us.

My feelings make me suspicious of Andromeda. Maybe on some level our intuition and feelings are a form of worthiness detection.

"I told Andromeda I would return her to her planet, Tarin, after I met with your people," I said and saw Andromeda perk up.

"Please, I want this nightmare to stop. I want to go home and pretend this is all a bad dream." Andromeda pouted meekly. Candy started to glow and growled softly toward her.

CHAPTER 11

Terrek

I stayed close to my mate as the Gias people came and went and buzzed around us with the intent to investigate the ship's technologies. I smelled females. All of them seem to be females, even the ones who wear uniforms that cover their heads and faces.

Battle-ready females, they all wield the power of the gods and the star people's technology. I smelled Darah and Flame, these two females have imprinted on my soul, and I will know their scent anywhere. I sense Flame has recognized Darah and I. She has given me a knowing glance, and I smell her arousal around us.

I needed to adjust and process all this myself. I was still learning about this vast universe. I had come to understand all of this was technology, advanced tools run by machines, and artificial intelligence. I was just trying to grasp the reality of this new world among the stars.

Darah has caught the eye of Flame. I'll follow Darah anywhere. She owns my heart. I can hardly believe that my bond mating will include two females who are more than I could ever be worthy of having.

Flame is formidable and fierce in her own right, based on my first impression. She oversees all the warrior women up here on the port dock.

I like to stand back, watch all these females talk, and make plans. The Andromeda female is being ignored until she can be scanned for worthiness, the chetaht is a dangerous animal, and he clearly doesn't like her.

I like these warrior females, and they impress me. I am glad that Darah has allies who are strong and smart, able to protect her and support my Darah, so I walk silently, just listening. I am always learning as I take in all the new things.

I can tell Darah is embracing the idea of our mate bond. I would love to take her away from all this to do the traditional newly bonded retreat. We could fully enjoy our new union. I was battling my need for her and also my need for Flame. I felt torn between happiness over my fated mates and sadness over my people and home planet.

I was haunted and driven to get my Laverian people freed of the Kanenites. Watching these warriors and seeing the advanced weapons had me eager to save my kind. I was eager to download the galaxtic empire educators as well, I must learn all I could.

Fame glanced my way; her eyes grew sultry just long enough for me to see before she caught herself and looked back on her task. I sensed she was fighting her own instinct to fuck us. My cock grew hard with need after that spell she cast on me with just a look. Both flame and Darah's arousal scent mingled in the air making me mad with lust.

I looked at a viewing screen and tried to calm my desire. Our earthling Darah needs to accept and embrace the union between us all before Flame and I can act on our bond.

Flame and I both were waiting for Darah to realize we all three were bonded. It was unspoken between us. I know Darah feels confused, and it just seems like it is not the time to explain how on rare occasions, there are mating between three or more souls that are fated with an unbreakable bonding.

The sudden alarm blaring from Flame's wrist was hurting my ears. I saw an image appear like magic above her wrist. She turned that blaring sound off, thankfully.

"A fleet of warships are approaching, surrounding our planet," a female face appeared as a hologram as she spoke to Flame.

"Put the shield in active defense mode and put the armed satellites on full attack sensors." Flame demanded as she rushed from the cargo area to exit our ship and go to her port command center.

This spaceport above the planet was remarkable. With its power grid and weapons ready to protect the planet and surface below. I wish my planet were this protected.

Darah looked at me, a bit nervous, as Candy bolted out of the doors, fully glowing his pastel colors.

"We need to keep an eye on him, Darah. He is still a wild predator."

She doesn't understand the viciousness of the chetaht. Somehow, she tamed him, barely, though, and I will never understand how. I had never heard of this before. I know she has claimed Candy, and so I have claimed him as well, even if he and I understand that we must tolerate each other for Darah's sake.

"I know Terrek, but I do trust him. Come on, we should check on him. He seemed worked up."

We rushed out of cargo and saw Candy attacking the command door, growling, glowing, hissing, and clawing at the metal door.

" Darah approached him cautiously. She makes me nervous. I readied myself to charge the chetaht if he showed aggression towards Darah.

"You should give him space," I said, hoping I wouldn't have to have a bloody fight with her pet.

"Candy, sweet boy! What has you throwing such a conniption fit?" Darah said in a soothing, sweet voice.

Candy let his fur dim as he huffed and hissed at the door. He paws at it and looks at Darah as if to ask her to open the door. Darah pulls out her device, I pull mine too.

"Put it on stasis for now. No need to kill just yet." Darah insisted.

I am glad to understand how to operate these devices now. Darah was confident, so that I would follow her lead.

Darah looked at me with a sassy wink. "Well, boys, let's see what has gotten Candy so upset." She used her thumb to open the command door.

Candy rushed past us and placed himself crouching in front of Andromeda, who was sitting in the corner holding her knees, crying.

How did you get in here, Andromeda?" Darah asked sternly.

Candy pointed his venomous tail spine at her. As he dimmed his fur, he looked at Darah as if begging for permission to kill Andromeda.

"Please take it away from me," Andromeda asked as she cried.

Crouching in a corner, hugging her knees. Trembling and hyperventilating, she tried to turn her head away from the snarling Candy.

"Candy, come here, boy. It's okay. Leave Andromeda alone."

He hissed and hopped over to Darah obediently.

"I do believe this girl is playing possum with us" Darah said as she looked at the female suspiciously.

"What is with his tail?" Darah asked, looking at me.

"Darah, he is a deadly apex animal. He has a venomous spine tail, he can sting over and over if he chooses, but in life threating attacks he can projectile one life-threatening stinger like a dart."

I looked at Andromeda suspiciously, I am with the beast on this matter, she is up to something.

He must feel like Andromeda is life-threatening if he is willing to let lose his dart on her. It is painful and takes a long time to regrow."

"Wow! You are full of surprises, Candy." Darah said soothingly while rubbing his big ears.

"No need to kill her just yet. Be a good boy and be nice for now." Darah continued baby-talking the deadly beast.

Candy glared at me, letting me know he was Darah's special beast.

I know she loves the beast, so I accepted this craziness of having a chetaht for a pet.

"Andromeda, how did you get into the command deck?" Darah asked again. She took steps to get Candy to move away from Andromeda.

She had stood up, looking timid and scared.

"I heard the commotion and all the soldiers leaving the ship, when I saw two of them leaving the command deck, I slipped in thinking I'd find you here and figure out what was happening.

I got scared when the doors closed, and this place was empty; I thought the Kanenites were back and coming to get me. Then I heard your pet trying to tear up the door to get to me." Andromeda's eyes brimmed with tears, and her lip trembled.

Candy Hissed and kept his tail aimed at her.

"Calm down, boy, it's okay, sweetie." Darah soothed Candy.

Darah approached her dash panel to see if anything was messed with. As the door slid open again, and two masked soldiers entered.

"Flame has requested that we escort all of you to her command center." A stern female voice said through the apparatus covering her face. Her voice sounded robotic.

"Okay, everyone, let's go see what all the fuss is about, Darah said.

Darah held my hand, and we all left the ship. Andromeda stayed feet behind us as Candy kept his tail pointed at her. The warriors took a guard on either side of her. She still has not been deemed worthy. I don't feel bad for the scared female because I don't smell the scent of fear on her.

"Maybe we should be extremely leery of this stranger female if the beast doesn't like her," I whispered to Darah.

"Oh, I already am Terrek," Darah said, reassuring me she hadn't fallen for those tears.

She squeezed my hand and glanced my way but said nothing as we walked along the nearly deserted port. As we walked, our footsteps seemed to echo with each step.

My gut knotted with a feeling of impending doom. Why my anxiety had gripped me all of a sudden, I did not yet know. My instinct was to grab Darah, find Flame, and get them somewhere safe.

I would not let Darah out of my sight, not until I know she was safe. Part of me was happy the deadly beast is so attached to my mate. I knew Candy would defend her if we needed to fight.

Seeing Flame as we entered her command station calmed my worry about her. At least the two of them were close enough that I could get to both of them if needed. Flame was busy directing her crew, monitors were up, the ceiling was a viewing image of another hologram.

I had never seen anything like it in all my life. We were in the outer atmosphere of the Gia's planet. The electric grid that surrounded the planet was now pulsing red. When we arrived, it was like a clear shield that shimmered, almost like a glass window.

The grid of satellites that held armed laser cannons sat outside the red pulsing shield surrounding the planet. The war pods were hovering in formation, making their own grid of pilots ready to defend the planet. These females were truly battle skilled.

I wished my world could have had a fighting chance. If we had a way of defending ourselves, we would have never been harvested. My mate was wise coming here for allies.

"How can we help?" Darah asked when Flame finally landed her red eyes in our direction.

"We discovered that the Kanenites were planning on attacking us since we are the closest galactic defense to their borders. Our star system had never surveyed the outer boundaries of our universe because we weren't aware that it existed. We haven't even discovered the class three planet's Laverian and Tarin yet. If it weren't for you and the Goddess Harmony, we would be ambushed without intel on our new enemy." Flame gave Darah a grateful gaze.

"Your ship sent a message with a radio wave we are unfamiliar with. it was sent out just minutes before our sensors picked up on the inbound invasion fleet. We are still trying to decipher the message," Flame said.

As she turned to address another alarm that beeped on the command monitor.

I felt Darah tense as she turned to face Andromeda. Candy's fur glowed as he snarled at Andromeda.

"Did you send the Kanenites a message? Is that why you were in my command center?" Darah asked in a low, calm tone.

The scared female backed up until she hit the wall, her hands out in a plea.

"No, I wouldn't know how. They kidnapped me. I have no reason to send them anything. I swear, please believe me."

Candy licked his fang and crouched. He looked up at Darah, waiting for permission to attack.

"No, Boy, not yet," Darah said, and those fangs lost their grin and hissed in disappointment.

"I am about to rattle that bitch bald myself!" Darah said in her angry southern accent.

Part of me wanted to see her fight the untrustworthy female. I like it when she is angry it was sexy to me.

Darah stared at her with true suspicion. Without looking away from Andromeda, she spoke loudly.

"Flame, can I ask that you have Andromeda detained in a holding cell until we get to the bottom of this message thing?"

"She has not been scanned for worthiness, agreed, take her now. I will deal with her after she is scanned." Flame said as two fully masked soldiers took Andromeda away.

I heard her crying about how unfairly she was being handled until the doors closed. Candy was completely relaxed, his tail swooshing and eager for Darah's attention.

"There's a good boy." Darah kissed him and hugged the deadly beast as he chuffed and purred.

We held hands and stood back when she stood up as we watched Flame coordinate her army for an attack.

Flame zoomed her view screen in on the space just beyond the reach of their laser cannon.

A grid of Kanenites crafts like the one Darah stole hovered still. Surrounding the Gias planet with its own formation that matched the defense setup of Gias. Battle lines were drawn and ready. My heart pounded, and fear crept in as I realized the Kanenites were incoming.

"Whatever happens, stay next to me, Darah. I love you. If this is the day I die, I will die fighting for you." I insisted. Darah gave me a tight hug and kissed me strongly.

"It's not that easy to get rid of me, big guy. Don't worry, Terrek, we are about to kick some serious ass. You'll see." This female amazes me.

"I'd like to see that," I said as I pulled her close to my side. I was still not taking any chances.

I kept an eye on Flame, trying to calculate the steps it would take for me to get to her. We may not have completed the bonds between us, but I will also protect her.

I saw the first wave of Kanenites fighter pods launching

toward the planet. On instinct, I stood before Darah and looked up at the viewing display on the ceiling.

The space laser cannons lit up the darkness of space. Firing at the enemy, the first of the Kanenites war pods exploded, but a few cleared the lasers and hit the red pulsing shield surrounding the planet.

I saw Flame standing confident and giving orders. I fought my need to collect her and shield both of my females. The Kanenites war pods that encountered the planet's shield bounced back into space with a blanket of electrical lightning, suffocating the entire war pod for a few moments until the pod imploded. The display of lights and colors was eerily beautiful. The lightning flew back into the protective shield, and the first strike terminated the invaders.

"They are testing our defenses." Flame said with a smirk.

This female was ready for battle; I could sense her eagerness. She was reveling with a battle high. I truly hope she was as capable as she was confident. Because I have seen my planet plucked dry of everything by these Kanenites.

I don't want that sorrow to replace this female's confidence. I am happy to have a fierce warrior join my life and be there to protect Darah. I will die for them. My nature wants me to shelter them away from danger. But the Gods saw fit to give me capable, stubborn females I know will not want me to shelter them as I wish to.

"How do you produce the power level to protect your planet?" Darah asked in awe.

My mate stepped out from behind me. She was still staring up at the viewing screen.

"We convert sunlight. We store our collected power to distribute throughout our planet, our atmosphere shield, our ships, and everything mechanical is powered by our sun."

"That's incredible!" Darah spoke.

"We have propulsion engines with core banks where the power runs for a thousand years before it needs to be plugged into a converter to recharge. Our shield and laser will outlast these Kanenites."

"Gias has magnificent warrior women." I praised.

"However, there is no need to wait them out. I have already requested assistance from our patrol fleet, which is inbound now. These fools are about to get their asses handed to them by our Galaxtic enforcers." Flame said with a grin, showcasing her broad white teeth where two dainty fangs popped out suddenly.

If these two beautiful females aren't the death of me, I will be surprised. I thought, eager to kiss Flame. I wanted her fangs to leave a mate mark on my other shoulder.

The viewing screen zoomed in on the outer perimeter where the Kanenites fleet surrounded the planet. Flame's face appeared on a screen before us as she stood tall and confident. Fierce with her teeth on display, she had a battle-ready expression.

"Hear me now, enemy, return to the hole you crawled out of or die; it is as simple as that." Flame's voice was menacing.

Damn, this female was sexy! I could smell that Darah was aroused as well as she looks at Flame with a blush creeping into her cheeks. I forced myself to concentrate on the fight and not these distracting females.

After she had finished her message, her image was closed from the viewing screen. Flame gave Darah and I a sultry glance before she focused on her display of viewing screens.

The ceiling viewing screen lit up with a space fighter fight surrounding the planet in a grid of fighters. The Galactic enforcer ships decloaked themselves and attacked.

Flame was right, in just under an hour the Kanenites were annihilated. Only a few were reported to have retreated successfully. One warship was being towed to port for interrogation.

Cloaked Galactic enforcers were tracking the retreating Kanenites to spy and collect intel.

I pulled Darah in for a hug and kissed her head.

"Mate, I am so thankful I have you," I whispered. Feeling very relieved that this battle was over for the time being.

We both kissed and focused on Flame, silently watching her work.

I wondered at that moment if Darah finally realized what Flame was to us.

I broke free from that steamy kiss. I saw Flame watching us, her eyes hooded in lust. She quickly adjusted and turned her attention back to the viewing screens. My palms sweated, and my heartbeat thrummed in my ears. I couldn't tell if my feelings resulted from his kiss or Flame's alluring gaze. I shook it off. This was not the time. Realizing we had won this battle, I shouted out loud.

"Yes! Woohoo! That's what I am talking about!"

In excitement, cheering on my new friends. The Gia›s female warriors kicked some serious ass. Flame had this look of confidence and pride that I admired.

"I am totally Team Flame. Remind me never to piss you off," I said as I held up my hand to high-five Flame.

She looked confused at the gesture. I sighed, feeling silly.

"What is Team Flame?" She asked. She gently grabbed my raised hand.

"It's an earth thing, which means I am on your side. This is called a high five. We clap hands in the air to celebrate. See, let me show you."

I took her hand and motioned her arm to high-five me. We practiced a couple of times, and her eyes lit up with amusement.

"I like you, little earthling." Flame said as she returned to focus on the incoming galactic enforcers.

"I like you too, Flame," I said to her back as I watched her work. I turned to glance at Terrek.

"She's smart as all get out, Flame is." I said to Terrek who pulled me back into his arms so I could lean on him as we both admired Flame.

I felt tingles looking at Flame. Something stirred inside me.

I looked up at my big purple man. Wondering if I should feel guilt for my attraction to Flame.

Terrek, do you want to return to our ship while we wait for things to settle?» I asked, needing to put a bit of distance between Flame and me.

I needed to clear my head and think. This was so confusing. His gorgeous smile and shining black eyes looked at me with hunger.

"Yes, mate, we shall go to our ship," Terrek said eagerly.

Candy rubbed against my thigh and chuffed.

"Okay, boys, let's get on home." Terrek was so handsome and powerful as his giant hand held mine.

I fed Candy a big hunk of meat from the food dispenser and took my big man to our room. His kiss melted away any lingering stress that I had. I held onto his horns and lost myself in his touch. I kissed him hungrily, gripping his horns as he lifted me in his arms. I was frantic to get naked.

I unzipped his uniform, and he helped me get out of mine. I laid back on the bed, exposed and spread for him. He growled and stared at me, scanning my body with his hungry black eyes. My sexy Terrek made my body catch on fire with desire.

You›re so pretty and pink like a flower.» He said just before he delved into the bed and kissed my clit.

"Oh, God!" I gasped as he made my whole body react to his magic tongue.

I went over the edge with ecstasy as he worked out one orgasm after another using his mouth and fingers. I held onto his horns as I bucked and ground my core into his devouring mouth. He used his mouth in a rhythm of circular pressure and gentle suction that had my clit sweal with sensitivity and my wetness slick his face.

I was in the arms of the male I love, an alien male. I found him utterly gorgeous as his purple hands gripped my thighs. In his arms, under his touch and kisses, I was swept away from my grief and my fears. Nothing mattered more than that moment of pure lovemaking.

When I thought I might die from too many orgasms, I pulled on his horns. His face released me with a wet pop. He was a sexy sight, crawling up my body to give me a juicy kiss. Tasting myself on his lips was sexy as hell.

I wrapped my legs around his hips, urging him to enter me. He slid his thick cock in fully inside me, and we both moaned in ecstasy as he rubbed the Knot at the base of his cock just right on my clit.

Terrek picked up the pace and pounded into me. His hard body was purple and sweaty, and the rhythm he used rubbed into my over-sensitive clit. My slick walls clamped down on him. I heard him moan deliciously.

"Mmmmm." as he bent down to nibble my earlobe. We came simultaneously as I felt him swell and fill me with his hot, pulsing seed.

"Darah, my love, I am beyond blessed to have you as my mate. Touching you is exactly what I needed tonight. I needed to feel you safe, sexy, and wholly mine. I will love you forever." Terrek whispered huskily in my ear.

Goosebumps rose across my flesh as I savored our bodies so intimately intertwined. He slowly got up and grabbed a warm, wet bathroom towel. He cleaned me and then himself. He was the sweetest, sweeter than cherry pie. Falling asleep in his arms, I felt happy and safe.

CHAPTER 12

Darah

As soon as I entered dreamland, I heard my mom singing her twangy "Bobby McGee" style while strumming the guitar. I got up and followed the sound. I found my mom in the chow hall sitting at a table. I sat in front of her, tearing up, and I saw how young and perfect she looked.

"It's not the same as when we sang around our fire pit back home, but it is sure good to see your sweet face again, Darlin." My mother said sweetly as she winked at me.

"Am I dreaming? Oh, Momma, I miss you so much." I said through tears. I pulled her into me for a hug. The guitar clanking between us. This felt so real.

"I know, pumpkin. We miss you too. I am so proud of you for finally getting up and doing right. You keep on with it, now, just as you are—no more wallowing. Ya here!" My mother sat back on the table.

"Your daddy, brother, and I were greeted by the great creator and introduced to the Goddess Harmony. She had offered Jason a place in her afterlife beyond the veil. The Great

Creator, our God, will allow your father and I to visit through your dreams, as he does with all who pass and enter his heaven. He said It wasn't supposed to be Jason's time, so he would grant him the choice to stay with us or go with Harmony." My mother beamed with pride telling me about her encounter with the gods.

"He took the good Goddess up on her offer as he wanted to see this amazing life you are making for yourself. Your daddy and I are with you, darlin, always. I'll keep this short and sweet as you have work to do dear." My mom kissed my cheek and stepped away before I could respond. I had so many questions. I saw my mother smiling at me as she faded away.

I woke up startled, as I didn't want to stop seeing my momma. Terrek pulled me close.

"Are you well, mate?" Terrek asked with a sleepy voice.

"Yes, love, I am. I dreamed of my mom and didn't want to stop seeing her just yet."

"I am so sorry for your loss, my heart. I wish I could go back in time and save them." Terrek kissed my forehead.

"Me too, big guy, me too." I kissed him softly and got out of bed.

Grabbing my guitar, I went to the chow hall to feed Candy and make my morning tea. I held my cup in my left hand, circling clockwise, letting the leaves settle. I drank as I focused on my future. I truly wanted to save Terrek's people and restore his planet.

I drank all but the last sip. I swirled the tea quickly from left to right before I flipped my cup over and set it down on the table. After a minute, I turned my cup back upright. I started near the handle of my cup. The shape of a skull and bones told me danger was present. The crushed truck at the other end of the cup reminded me of my past when my family died. I swallowed that lump of raw grief to continue my reading.

On the side, I saw war in my future. At the bottom, I saw three hearts. I was unsure how to interpret all that information, but I was glad to be settling back into my old routine.

This ritual calms me and centers me for the day. I was running low on my black loose-leaf tea leaves. I shook my zip lock baggy. I needed to find a proper alternative soon.

Well, that's an uneasy feeling to wake up to. I took my guitar and started playing my music, singing my favorite toons from Earth.

Terrek paused, eating to watch me sing. Even Candy seemed to wag his tail as I sang; I felt the vibe of the music and something familiar from my home. These two had no idea how much I loved them. How much was my life better with them in it? I let myself retreat into the song, giving me a moment to face the day. My mind flashed images of Flame and her sexy smile, and my heart fluttered. I tried to shake that giddy feeling off.

"Y'all better stay close today, boys. My tea said to be vigilant," I said as we left our ship to find Flame.

The dock was busy this time, and war pods were parked and stacked on either end. The bay was filled with pods that were getting repaired. Through the atmosphere shield keeping the vacuum of space out of the docking area, I could see the planetary protection still glowed red. Beyond that, a towing ship collected all the imploded enemy crafts floating around the space outside. this time, I had not heard my footsteps as we walked toward the command center.

"Hi, Flame. It looks like you have another busy day," I said as we greeted my new sexy friend.

My gut tightened, and I realized I had felt butterflies whenever I saw Flame. I looked at Terrek; I felt butterflies for him, too. What was happening?

"Yes, I am just tidying up some things. I am sending the debris from our battle to our fire, the star. The tow ship is hooking the collection to a drone that will hit the sun. As soon as I launch the drone, we must head down to the surface to test Andromeda for worthiness."

I needed to file the butterflies away and focus on the day ahead. Me being smitten over Flame was too much to analyze at that moment. I needed to get to the bottom of this Andromeda situation.

"Clever, I like how you take the time to clean up the space debris," I mentioned in awe as I watched the drone blast off on its way to the sun with white light, leaving a trail behind it as it flew away.

Flame looked sensuous with her red eyes and satisfied smile. I knew we were going to be great friends. I was so drawn to her. Seeing her dark red hair pulled back in a tight braid. I had the urge to untie it to see her hair fall freely.

Whoa! What was going on with me? I held Terrek's hand as Candy stayed on my left thigh. We followed Flame to the jump ship to see about Andromeda on the surface.

Candy laid at my feet; a bit nervous with the turbulence from the jumper ship on our trip down. I rubbed his big ears, and he mellowed out, adapting to the new sensation. We entered the council hall, and at that time, Andromeda was already strapped into the worthiness detector machine chair.

The raised chairs before the audience were full of the females who sat before us the last time we were here. Empress Zion entered the room and sat at the center, facing Andromeda in the chair. We stood along the wall with Flame.

Empress lowered her red gaze at the soldier standing behind the worthy chair.

"Proceed." She said, and we watched as the lights dimmed, and Andromeda's whimpers went silent.

A hologram surrounded her and her chair. Like a scene from a movie in three dimensions. Andromeda was standing on the captain's command deck on a ship, looking at a viewing screen of the planet Tarin. My heart sank when I saw her wearing a Kanenites commander uniform.

"Did you get all of it?" she had asked as she zoomed her screen in on the planet, showing that the Kanenites had already invaded Tarin and were harvesting the last of the resources, much like they did on Laverian.

"Yes, Commander Edge, we are wrapping things up. I have those females you requested. I will send them up to you now."

"I expect them soon." The commander's cold tone snapped as she closed the viewing screen. Little men scrambled out of her way as she left her command center and went to the cargo area.

"Get these vile things off my ship already." She yelled as she gazed at the Laverian men floating in stasis. I felt Terrek tense as we watched the memories displayed in the hologram before us.

The timid, tearful Andromeda was gone. Only a brutal, evil commander showed her true nature before us. My stomach felt queasy watching it. The Laverian men were being transferred to another ship. The next was a load of Laverian females. We watched as more animals and resources were removed.

Soon, several females were delivered to Commander Edge. They were stripped naked and presented to Andromeda, who circled them and inspected them disdainfully.

"Is this the best you could find?" She scoffed to the small man who presented the traumatized females.

"Unfortunately, I am afraid this planet doesn't have very impressive specimens, Commander Edge." The little man shrugged, unimpressed.

"I have inspected and chosen the best available females for you, Commander Edge." He said with a sparkle in his eye.

"So be it. Clean them up, collar them, and place them in the pods. I will give them to my father. He can use or discard them as he wishes. I will retire to a pod myself. Don't bother to wake me until we return." Her pig like ears ruffled in agitation as she spoke.

Andromeda Edge left the females and the little man. She headed to the pods and undressed. She lay down as the AI machines gave her injections and applied monitors, putting her into stasis. When she woke, she was disoriented.

Andromeda saw the blinking light displaying the date and time.

"Those imbeciles must have done something wrong to wake me too soon." She whispered through clenched teeth. She noticed an unknown female approaching her pod.

"Enough!" Empress Zion said the hologram disappeared as the lights came on.

Candy›s fur and hunched posture lit up, and growls filled the air as Andromeda became aware again.

"Down, boy," I said as I rubbed his ears. She resumed her tears and trembling as she begged.

"Please, I am not bad. I want to go home."

Candy's hackles rose again his fur glowing and a low growl began. "Hold your horses Candy, I don't like her but we are gonna be nice for now."

The Empress raised her brow.

"Andromeda Edge, you have been deemed unworthy." The Empress declared as she stood." Take her to the interrogation cells."

All the humility disappeared from Andromeda's features, and she let out a menacing laugh.

"Fools, you have no idea what you are up against. You don't know who I am, but you will." She said like she had a pot to piss in.

"Fuck around and find out! Up till now, I've been forgiven and forgetting because of the way I was raised, but I'll tell you one thing, if it was up to me, I'd let Candy eat your ass, as I had promised. You better hope your fate lies in the Gias hands." I shouted after Andromeda as she was being hulled out.

The soldiers sedated her, and she fell into stasis as they took her to be interrogated. I was left spitten mad with my Candy still glowing, and I felt Terrek wrap me in his arm shaking with a booming laughter.

"Darah, you amaze me, fierce little human."

CHAPTER 13

Darah

The Empress's features softened when she saw us standing at the wall.

"Please join me for a meal," she said as she moved to exit the council room. Flame guided us in meeting the Empress in the hallway.

"Now, I regret not letting Candy eat her! What will happen to her now?" I whispered as we began to walk.

"She will be interrogated, and if she doesn't have anything valuable to share, she will be executed." Flame explained.

"She deserves an Oscar with her damsel in distress acting job she gave us," I can't believe I ever felt sorry for her even a tad.

"If receiving this Oscar means she suffers as much as she caused suffering, then yes, she deserves the most painful Oscar." Flame agreed.

I giggled a little and decided not to explain the meaning of the Oscar awards ceremony.

"She knows where they took my people." Terrek said with

a somber tone. Flame stopped and looked at Terrek with compassion.

"I will find your people, Terrek, I will fight to get them rescued and returned home." Flame vowed. She reached for Terrek and then pulled back before touching him.

Terrek's black eyes looked at Flame with true emotion. They just had a moment. It was tender, and I liked how it made me feel to watch them together in their moment. I felt saddened that Flame held back. We followed the Empress and her escorts to a dining area on another level of the tall building. The table had already been set up as a banquet table.

"Please, sit. We shall share this meal and discuss the Kanenites." The Empress motioned us to the table.

Empress Zion took her seat at the end of the table. Masked soldiers held our chairs out as we sat on the side next to the Empress. Plates of food and drinks were placed in front of us.

"We will extract information from Andromeda Edge and the other spacemen. We are gathering information from their ships as we sit here and eat. Worry not. We will get your Laverian people back." The Empress looked directly into Terrek's sad black eyes.

"Thank you, Empress Zion," Terrek said as he bowed his head and placed his hand over his heart.

I took a bite of the stew that was in front of me and moaned out loud.

"This is so delicious, put that on the top of your head and your tongue would beat your brains out trying to get to it." I said. I had never tasted anything so good before. I was from Texas and proud of our smoked barbeque. I never imagined an alien stew would steal my heart.

The Empress let out a soft laugh. I blushed with embarrassment , but I just couldn't help myself. You can take a country girl to space and all that but you can't take the country outta the girl.

Yes, it is one of my favorites as well.» She said as she took her bite.

Everyone started to eat. As we enjoyed the food. I took in the modern, sleek, opulent décor. The dinnerware was dark and pristine. They had a two-prong fork made of stone, a spoon with a curved handle, and a stone-gripped knife.

This all felt so out of my country girl league. I was used to backyard bonfires with Texas barbeque or takeout. I thought the food replicator was impressive. All this was way out of my element. The servers dressed in fancy black uniforms and they were quick to keep food and drinks coming. I had to fight the urge to get up and help them. The lighting was bright and I felt surprisingly comfortable among the group as we ate formally with a casual ease. We began to talk about the Kanenites.

"From what I understand, the Goddess Harmony has a true mate, a God named Hecat. He is the God who created all of you and your universe. Harmony has recently married him. She has become aware of his creations and is not happy. "

I took another bite of alien yumminess as I explained.

"The Goddess Harmony thinks her Hecat has been a God. He created this universe with all the different planets without checking on them or caring for his creations as he should have.

Harmony is not happy about her mate's neglect. She has picked me to help her set things right." I rolled my eyes, thinking that I was sounding like the porchlight was on but nobody was home kinda crazy.

"I hope I can help. I am unsure why I was chosen, but I will do my best." I glanced at Terrek and then Flame and realized I was grateful.

"The God of war, Kane, has created his universe. He took advantage of Hecat's neglect and invaded this universe."

"At first, I did not believe any of this. I thought I had died or was in a coma, but I finally came around. I am here and have whatever insight the Goddess Harmony has given me."

I looked at Terrek and smiled, grateful I had him.

"Terrek claims we are bond mates or true mates. On Earth, the closest connection to this kind of soul-binding love was marriage. I feel married to Terrek. I am getting used to calling him my mate instead of my husband."

"Ya'll are the good guys in Hecat's universe according to the insight the Goddess Harmony has given to me. She comes to me in my dreams. I remembered some of the things she had explained while I was sleeping. These Kanenites are from another universe altogether. The Gods have their own laws and are supposed to stick to their creations and in their own territory." I felt a blush creep up my cheeks as so many eyes were on me, listening with fascination.

"So, this God Kane is doing a huge no, no. I assume you have not mapped out anything further than your universe. The planet Tarin and Laverian are on the edge of Hecat's universe, so the God Kane has trespassed and allowed his creations to invade and harvest resources." I tried to explain something hard for me to comprehend.

"Harmony has her own mini-universe with just one planet sustaining life. Now that she is in the veil of the Gods and no longer in her own world, she wants balance restored and justice for the Hecat universe. She feels responsible as Hecat's true mate." I felt odd trying to speak on Harmony's behalf.

"It may not be our universe. This Kane's territory. It does not matter. We are now aware and will go after our own." The Empress said, seemingly not impressed by the gods.

"Exactly!" I smiled at her.

I am unsure how I feel about Kane or Hecat, but I trust Harmony. She is the only God with my loyalty at the moment.» I said confidently about my Goddess.

"Laverian and Tarin are class two and three planets, and we have strict laws preventing us from interfering. However, these Kanenites think they should avoid our laws. Now that they have harvested these worlds. We need to assimilate a new reality for them.

We will need to assess the dangers of the Kanenites and see if these planets can handle introducing some of our technology and knowledge to upgrade the primitive planets to class seven.

It is an exception we must make. So close to Kane's borders, "Empress Zion explained.

"Makes sense to me, momma always said you can't put the toothpaste back in the tube. These planets now know about space travel." I agreed.

"Every Galactic planet class five and above has an emperor or empress to represent that world. I represent this training base for the Gia's females. I propose you and Terrek of Laverian be the Emperor and Empress of the galactic forces for Laverian."

I looked at Terrek. "Do you want to represent Laverian with me? What will your people think?" I asked.

"My world was harvested. It might be too late to represent. I will accept this title for now if we accomplish saving my kind. I will revisit this role and see if my people accept this of me."

"Agreed and we will save your people," I said, determined to save Laverian for Terrek.

"It is settled. Welcome to The Galactic Empires of the Hecat's Universe." Empress Zion said with a proud smile, her red eyes shining.

"Flame, I will assign you to Terrek and Darah to upgrade Laverian's assimilation to the Galactic Empire." Empress Zion ordered.

"Yes, Mom." Flame responded; her sultry gaze focused on me.

"Yes, Empress Zion. Excuse my informal slip.

"Child, I see you are distracted. No need for formalities. We are not officially on duty, dear. All is forgiven. I will speak with you all soon." Empress Zion rose from the table and left us to finish up.

"I think it is time we upgrade your ship and deal with the lives you have stored in that cargo dock. Darah, I will give you a Galactic ship. That is far superior to the Kanenites ship you stole. " Flame suggested as she was getting right to work.

"I want to keep my stolen ship. It symbolizes my first steps toward getting myself on the right path. To live in a way to honor my family who passed." I said.

Flame cupped my face. I felt the need to rub my head into her hand. I forced myself to smile at her as I maneuvered back, I bent down to pet Candy.

"I understand how you are attached." Flame said sweetly.

"I'd like to find a place on the surface so Candy can stretch his legs since we were on the surface. Is there a place he can run for a bit before we head back up?"

I looked at Flame, who smiled brightly back at me. My heart fluttered loudly under the beam of her gaze.

"Of course, follow me." Flame said.

I smiled at Empress Zion. I was somewhat unsure of my new Empress title. I had never been shittin' in high cotton in my life, the title Empress seems like a lie. But, I am very grateful to Empress Zion for her support. I stood to follow Flame.

"Thank you, your majesty." I look forward to working with you and for the Galactic Empires."

She smiled, "No need to be so formal when we are not in an official meeting or event. I look forward to knowing you better, Empress Darah. After all, we are practically Family now. Once things settle, we will arrange a proper coronation on your planet, Laverian. " Empress Zion looked at Flame affectionately.

"I have a feeling I will be getting to know you and Terrek a lot better here in the near future." Her smiling eyes looked at me as if she knew a secret I wasn't privy to yet.

"Looking forward to it," I said taken aback as we walked away.

Terrek grabbed my hand as we followed Flame. Flame took us to a hover transport, and we glided it toward the training field.

"This is a wild training field where we send our recruits once they have advanced to test their survival skills in case they crash or need to be covert in wild conditions." Flame looked at Candy, eagerly looking out the window, purring and chuffing with his tail wagging happily.

"We just had a graduation for our advanced recruits who made it through training, so this area is clear for now. It is safe for him to hunt and run."

Flame stopped the hover transport, and we all exited. Feeling the outside air and the breeze on my face had me relax and truly take in the moment of being on another new planet. I was thrilled it wasn't hotter than all get out this time.

The air was rich and clean with oxygen, so much so that it reminded me of an oxygen bar I once used at a mall. Candy sniffed the air, He bolted as he hopped-ran fast. The pure delight Candy had out in nature filled me with giddiness. I would make it a point to find nature so he could stretch his legs and run as he should.

I picked up a stick to see if he would play fetch. To my delight, he loved to fetch.

"That's a good boy!" I cheered him on as we played for hours. Flame and Terrek took turns throwing the stick for a very playful Candy. We all seemed caught up in the delightfulness of being outside together in peace.

"Darah, you amaze me," Terrek said as he held me from behind as Flame played fetch with Candy.

"I never could have imagined playing with a Chetaht and having a good time amid all the worry I carry for my planet and my kind. Being here with you, somehow, I feel like I can face anything as long as I have you by my side." Terrek confided in my ear.

The sky grew darker, and Flame walked close to us as she dusted herself off.

"I cannot remember the last time I laughed this much. Thanks to you two, I have had a much-needed reprieve from my duties." Flame said with a saucy wink.

Candy chuffed, ran to Terrek and rubbed Terrek's thigh affectionately.

"Really? Candy?" Terrek asked, surprised as he knelt

down, petting Candy's big ears. I stepped away from them to give my boys a chance to bond.

"That's sweet." Flame leaned in and whispered to me as I stood next to her to watch.

"They look like two peas in a pod, I knew they'd eventually warm up to each other. Melts my heart. I love seeing Terrek happy. He deserves a good life. I intend to help him have that." I said.

"I will help you. I joined the Galaxy Force to do good and save people. I can't stand a tyrant. These Kanenites have no honor." Flame vowed.

"I cannot express how grateful I am to know you and have your support and friendship, Flame."

"I understand, and those boys must get used to me." Flame said with a smile.

That smile melted something inside me. I took a deep breath as tingles heated throughout my body. I turned to look at my boys playing.

"I am sure we all will love having you around more," I said once I collected myself. Flame smiled as she watched the boys play.

"We need to leave soon." She said, looking at her wrist device. Flame had taken her form-fitting uniform jacket off and wore a casual black tank top underneath.

Seeing her skin and her body in this revealing undershirt, caused heat to flush my cheeks as arousal thrums like a heartbeat at my core. I tried to deflect that reaction and mention her alien-like tattoos.

"I like your golden tattoos. It looks like moving metal is under the surface of your skin."

Flame put her uniform jacket back on to cover her markings. For the first time, I saw a shadow of insecurity in Flames' features.

"I am sorry. I meant no offence to ya Flame."

"No, Darah, it's me. I had an injury that should have retired me from my service requirements. Instead, I decided to get an experimental surgery that gave me implants. The marking is an unavoidable display of my disability." Flame seemed embarrassed.

My people are not very accepting of weakness. I have to prove my worthiness constantly. Some think that because my mother is Empress Zion, I am somehow getting a special exception for my title as commander."

Flame laughed. "If they truly knew my mother, they'd never assume I would be treated with special liberties. In fact, my mother expects more of me than anyone else."

"I was enjoying the day so much. I just didn't think you would notice my markings, and now that you have, I worry you will think less of me for my markings. As they are proof, I needed a procedure to function properly again."

I wanted to pull her in for a hug and kiss her senselessly, bringing back that sultry gaze of hers.

"Fuck those judgmental assholes! From what I have seen, you are a badass package of awesome! You are a worthy woman to me, Flame.

My mom would say you're handicapable, not disabled. I think your markings are beautiful. On Earth, people would flock to get tattoos that flow like golden liquid. You should flaunt it like a badge."

Flame Smiled. "I am not sure of some of your Earth Speech, but I understand. Thank you for seeing me and not judging me."

Damn, I have to stop myself from kissing her. I thought I needed to have a candid conversation with Terrek soon. His gorgeous smile and shining black eyes looked at me with hunger as he and Candy walked back towards us.

"Shall we go to our ship? I am a bit hungry now." Terrek said eagerly as he walked up to Flame and me.

Candy rubbed against my thigh and chuffed.

"Okay, boys, let's get on home."

CHAPTER 14

Darah

We returned to my ship and went to the cargo area to the wall of the life pods. After scanning the inventory, we found that Andromeda had collared and collected the four females. The AI arms then placed the four pods on the main floor.

"Here we go," I said as I initiated the pods to open and wake the four females collared and stolen from the planet Tarin.

Flame and I had laid blankets on them and had clothes ready, folded, and placed over the end of the pods.

"Don't be afraid, ladies. We are here to rescue y'all." I tried to say in a soothing voice.

Hoping the universal translator Harmony gifted to me worked in Tarin languages, too.

These women were so much like Earth females. Fearful eyes woke up one by one and became aware. The redhead with long curly hair and green eyes, her freckled face, and dark skin. Sat up, her confused, sleepy, beautiful face morphed into absolute terror when her eyes landed on Terrek.

"Woah, it's okay, sweetie. He won't harm you." I looked at Terrek and my Candy.

"Terrek honey, please take Candy away for now. I think ya'll might be a bit too scary for these ladies as soon as they wake up, and settle, I'll introduce them later."

"Allow me to release you from those stupid collars." I offered as Terrek stepped back with his hands raised palm out.

"I mean no harm. I will take Candy to the chow hall. Be careful, Darah." Terrek gave me a slight nod and then he looked at Flame. They had some silent exchange. Then he turned and left with Candy.

Flame and I took a few steps back, allowing the female's the room to get up freely and out of the pods as they needed.

"Hello, my name is Darah, and this is Flame. We are here to help." I tried to explain to the scared females.

The redhead slowly exited the pod, holding the blanket on her.

The short-haired, Pixie-looking lady with wide brown eyes crawled out of her pod to get next to the tall redhead, who tried to place herself in front of the others.

"This one is the natural leader of these women." Flame whispered behind me.

I stood back, trying to look as friendly as possible. The third female was short and curvy and had shoulder-length, natural, curly black hair. Her light blue eyes popped in contrast to her ebony skin.

The last female was petite and thin. Her long, straight, jet-black hair fell past her waist. She had golden light brown eyes and she crouched behind the short, curvy dark lady. They all stood behind the redhead, as they stared at Flame and me with fear. I pulled the collar control device out of my back pocket.

"Here, let me help you get those collars off?" I asked as I slowly approached the redhead. She stood still, glowering at me with untrusting eyes.

"I get it, and I don't expect you to accept that we are the good guys, not without proof," I said as I released the redhead from that slaver collar.

I held the collar in my hand and showed her how to use the device to lock and unlock the collar. Without words, I handed the device to the redhead, who took it, looking at me skeptically.

"Please, release your friends." I stepped back with Flame and watched the redhead as she released her friends.

"You see, even these females want us to prove our worthiness before they freely trust. I will like these Tarinites." Flame whispered.

Flame stood beside me, with her intense evaluation of the ladies.

"Okay, you may have a point, but try not to scare them." I agreed with Flame.

"I am Darah, and I stole this ship from the Kanenites spacemen. I was trying to save myself, my mate, and my fur baby, Candy when I took this spaceship.

These assholes harvested our planet too. We would have been left for dead if we did not escape." I looked at the ladies, who stood taller as they listened.

"This is my friend Flame. She is a badass warrior woman willing to help us fight these Kanenites." Flame allowed me to introduce her, but she still showed her aloof demeanor when she met new beings that hadn't been proven worthy yet.

"I often wondered if aliens existed. I am sorry to know that answer now." The redhead said as she let her green eyes scan her surroundings.

"You have no idea how much I understand. I was recently exposed to the technology and world of space travel." I said, trying to connect with the redhead.

"I can introduce yawl to the things that I have discovered. We can learn the rest together as we move forward." I suggested trying to gain a bit of trust.

I activated a viewing screen to show the females how I took

the ship and to show the recording of the Kanenites harvesting Laverian. Flame and I walked away to give them time to dress and watch the viewing. Eventually, the females approached us as we stood near the cargo door.

"My name is Jannali." The redhead introduced herself. Her dainty pointed ears poking through her hair.

The tiny female with long jet-black hair introduced herself next.

"My name is Aya." Her golden-brown eyes were still cautious.

The curvy female with bright, contrasting blue eyes stepped forward.

"You may call me Sade." She said with a raspy voice.

The Brunette with dark brown eyes said. "I am Leilani." Her fearful eyes broke my heart.

"I sure hate meeting you all under these circumstances. However, I promise to help you, and I hope we can become good friends." I said, meaning every word.

"Flame and I wanted to give you a tour, show you how things work, so let's get you fed and assign each of you, you're very own rooms. You have a choice here on this ship in the crew quarters, or you can go to the surface of Gias, and they will set you up a place to live until we can return you to your planet Tarin." I explained.

We showed the females around to let them get used to things and adapt before introducing them to Terrek and Candy. Much less a brand-new planet that was designed for war training.

These Tarinites females reminded me of home on Earth so much that it was easy to bond with them. Time will allow them to trust me in return. The ladies decided to stay on my ship for the meantime, after a few days on the ship, learning what I could teach them, they adapted very quickly.

Terrek and I trained them on how to work with the new technology by showing them and giving them the opportunity to download information with the educator. They had the option to stay safely on Gia's planet until we could get them home to Tarin safely.

Flame had the worthy chair installed on the ship, she insisted. After the females felt comfortable, they sat in the chair, determined to be worthy. Three of the females chose to train and to get ready to battle the Kanenites.

Aya wasn't a warrior and just wanted to stay safe until she could go home. She loved to garden, so after the females were deemed worthy, she was accepted as a refugee and given an area to garden on the planet Gias.

Terrek and I train as recruits. "A good leader will be trained just as those they lead." Flame insisted.

"I will gladly train. I have room for more markings. "Terrek offered proudly.

"I can't believe I survived that boot camp," I said as I was finally allowed to kiss Terrek after we endured a few weeks of hard training.

"I don't think I could have survived another day without touching you, my mate. I am glad we have accomplished war training, too." Terrek kissed me long and hard.

Flame beamed with pride as she took Terrek and me to the side.

"You two are very impressive, and you went through training hard and fast. Most recruits would not have been able to achieve graduation at the rate we put you through. Tarin, Laverian, and Earthlings are impressive indeed."

Flame, was genuinely happy and proud for all of us.

"Please enjoy tonight and tomorrow and get to know your newly upgraded ship. We have a meeting with Empress Zion tomorrow night." Flame said as we boarded the jump ship to transport us to the atmosphere entry port.

CHAPTER 15

Terrek

My heart is whole. "Darah, you have spellbound me." She was an enchantress.

"Terrek, I have not put a spell on you." She giggled.

"I love your accent; it's so sultry to me," I said.

I gazed at her kissable lips aching for her to speak again.

"It's called a southern drawl. I can't help it, I am a Texas gal."

"Texas must be a magical land to have produced my Darah," I mentioned as I watched her make her habitual tea.

"Texas was home. The magic was my family. It lives in my memory now. Being here with you is magic to me now, Terrek. you are my family." Darah said with sadness in her eyes.

I did not mean to remind her of the loss of her family. My own sadness surfaced when I thought of my family and the unknown of whatever the Kanenites were inflicting on them.

"I love you, my Darah." I leaned down to kiss her head while she looked at her tea leaves.

She was so cute with her morning teas and her Earth music.

Watching her hold her cup and intently stare at her leaves was a ritual that I found myself enjoying.

We sat in a garden just outside the council building, which was scented with blue and white blooms that grew over the pergola seating area. Everything in the air felt refreshing, and hope pulsed through my being.

Our training was not easy, and my Darah did not complain. Not even when I saw the pain in her eyes, she pushed through. I am very impressed by my Darah and the other females.

"Umm," Darah sighed as she read her fortune.

She was deep in thought, so I sat there silently supporting her.

I am proud of the calm and accepting way I have adapted to all the new knowledge, space travel, and the fact that aliens exist. I am glad to have allies who could help me fight this upcoming battle.

I hoped one day I could show Darah the village of our people, and she would love our home there. My home would become the new chief house when my father officially retired. I needed to save all of them and hoped they would find me worthy.

My sweet mate had not seen how great Laverian was. She was fighting for my people and my planet. She barely knows anything of my world but was solely dedicated to saving it. Darah only knew of the silence in the jungle, of suffering, being wet and cold and hungry.

There were so many wonders and beauty she had yet to discover, and I prayed for a future where I could share all the things that I love about my world with her. With both of my beautiful mates.

Flame, my other bond mate-to-be, has vowed to battle. I could not have had a fuller heart. The Gods had shown me favor with my two alien females.

Thank the Goddess Harmony for bringing me, my true mates. I couldn't have dreamed of better mates. Darah is more than I ever deserve. I will follow her anywhere.

Flame was fierce, with a greatness about her. She was gorgeous as a woman, bigger than life as a leader, and formidable as a warrior. She could be a legend among the stars. I just knew it in my soul. The way we could combine as a family and the possibilities that lay before us were endless. I could have never imagined it for myself. I was truly a blessed man.

"It's time to go to the council hall, my love." I stood and held my hand out to Darah.

"Oh, yes, sorry, I was caught up in the leaves. I think we will be meeting someone important soon." Darah grabbed my hand, I helped her up, and we walked into the council hall for our official meeting with Empress Zion.

The seats were packed with people. Flame waved us to the front row of seats. We sat next to her and the Tarin females.

"Are we late?" I asked, wondering if we were holding up the meeting.

"Almost." Flame said, giving me an irritated glance.

"Sorry, Flame." I stared at the fire in her eyes until they turned heated another way.

"Well, it's all my fault I got distracted," Darah told Flame with a blush.

"You're lucky I saved you a seat. No harm done. I was hoping to chat with you before the meeting." Flame teased with a wink.

Flame was angry or amused, and I was unsure. I did not want to anger her. She was formidable, and I have much respect for her. I found her sexy either way. If she was mad, Then I may have to find a creative way to rile her up from time to time.

It must have been hard for her to hold back her instinct. Our mating bond was unanswered, and it was not natural. I was finding my urges for Flame, harder and harder to resist.

Darah was already bonded with me. She was an Earthling and didn't seem aware of the mating call between all of us. I will need to find a good moment to discuss this with her. I did not want to upset her with my affection and desire for Flame.

The need to consummate our bond with Flame was beginning to be maddening.

"Introducing The Galactic Empire, her Majesty Empress Zion of Gias." A female bellowed, silencing the audience as Empress Zion walked into view.

The Empress wore a formal uniform and had her gray hair tight in a braid. She presented powerfully as she took her raised seat and sat.

"Greetings, warriors of the Galactic Empires. I have summoned you here this morning to declare war on the enemy known as the Kanenites. Our intel has introduced us to a new universe. The Kanenites have declared war on us by invading two of our class three planets."

The lights dimmed as a hologram filled the space above our heads and displayed a 3-D star system map.

"As you can see, this is the universe of the Kanenites system." Empress Zion zoomed in on a giant gas planet with several moons that had atmospheres rotating around the orange and yellow giant.

This moon is where the atmosphere is inhabitable for life; the Kanenites have residential outpost housing here. They use jumper ships to transport the warriors to and from the slaver prison moons, for every shift rotation."

The Empress zoomed to another moon. "As you can see, the slaver's Assimilation Stations have hostile atmospheres. Each moon is a prison for newly acquired enslaved people. "Empress Zions's face grew menacing with angry features as she continued her presentation.

"This moon is for the females." A large moon was zoomed in on where the surface showed buildings." It was a greyish moon with an atmospheric terraforming unit that made the environment barely sustainable.

"The elements are hazardous outside, a grey soft sandy stone for a surface. An atmospheric shield secures the buildings on this moon. We shall refer to this as target A. We shall rescue the females here and deliver them to the medical city ship that will be extremely defended nearby."

The view was dispersed, replaced by a three-dimensional blueprint of the building on the moon target A. The females were housed in bunks that gave no room to sit in. They were locked in unless they were able to shower and take the rehabilitation courses that shocked and tortured them into conversion and obedience.

I lost my breath and gasped in shock and fear at the realization. I needed to get to my people immediately. I had to stop myself from leaving my seat.

"From the information retrieved from the Kanenites ship and our spies, we learned that each building was designed to train enslaved people for that building's expertise.

Sex slaves here. Childcare enslaved people here. Service enslaved people here," The Empress zoomed in on each building.

"All despicable and against Galactic laws. This is Kanenites territory, and we have no authority there. However, these Kanenites drew first blood when they crossed our borders, stole our defenseless people, and harvested our protected planets."

Empress Zion looked fierce. Her body grew, her eyes blazed red, her nails grew into black claws, and her tiny canine fangs grew long and sharp. I felt fear as her energy went out in a wave of determination. Her transformation was a shock.

I growled as I glanced at where the females were imprisoned. Darah squeezed my hand. "We will rescue them," I promised with a whisper.

Target Moon B. was zoomed in on next. "This is the male's prison and assimilation camp."

The surface was fire and magma. The males are housed in a tall mountain above the lava and fire. They were collared with a sedation pump and electric shocks to manage the men.

"They are brutally trained for fighting entertainment. A sport that the Kanenites bet on. Men not passing the evaluation are sent to the meat market to be harvested and made into animal food."

A gasp erupted as the hologram zoomed in on a slaughterhouse for the disqualified men.

My eyes filled with tears, and anger vibrated throughout my body. Darah grabbed my hand harder. Flame rubbed my shoulders in concern.

"Some prisoners belong to the Kanenites universe. It has been decided by the Galactic Empire that we will offer all these prisoners refugee status, and they can live on any planet they choose within our universe."

"This is an immense undertaking. Laverian and Tarin must be reinforced and upgraded to a class seven planet. We will establish a border defense line between the Kanenites universe and our own. Since Laverian and Tarin are in our universe, they are our responsibility, even if unnoticed until recently. The Kanenites universe borders our universe by these two planets."

"The prison moons are on the edge of the Kanenites universe, allowing us to travel quickly from Laveriane space. We shall start our line of defense from there." Empress Zion stared over the collective audience.

The energy in this room felt palpable. I don't think the Kanenites were ready for this fight.

CHAPTER 16

Darah

"We have a planet in our system that turns to ice most of the annual cycle around our central star. The inhabitants must retreat to space to survive during the warm seasons. Our galactic empire has helped to build a massive space city that is situated like a moon around the ice planet Frio."

"The Frio people adapt to space and can walk with minimal protection. They engineer and build many of our outer space defenses and detection shields. Like the one around Gia." Flame said as she scrolled through the hologram screen on her wrist.

"You mean the Frio people can withstand the pressure of space?" I asked, blown away by the thought.

"They are resilient, naturally living in freezing temperatures. Their body can pressurize to deep depths and space. They are solid but fragile in heat. So, they wear a layer of sun-flare-resistant clothes and can hold their breath using the oxygen in their blood to feed their body when they spacewalk.

It gives them the agility to construct and build in space efficiently and fast.

We delivered supplies and protection while they engineered and constructed for us or our galactic planets. So, I have commissioned the Frio people to come with their portable cities to Laverian and Tarin to make a defense shield similar to Gia. Because these planets are on the border of Kane's universe."

Flame was lost with her wrist hologram: "I have handpicked a crew for us on your ship, Darah. Did you name her yet?"

"Stealth, Davis," I said proudly as we walked with the crowd leaving the council room.

"That is a nice way to honor your family," Flame said as I rubbed my thumb back and forth while we held hands.

"Great! I officially logged your ship's new name into our system. We need to ascend to the port and ensure last minute supplies are stalked. I will do pre-launch checks with you to review our upgrades." Flame tore her gaze away from the hologram to make eye contact with Terek and me as he stood beside me.

I was glad we are moving forward to fight and save all those people.

After a long day and evening of preparing my ship. I fell asleep and was happy to visit with my family in my dream. I was glad I didn't dream of that crash anymore. The burnt engine and asphalt smell haven't tortured my soul for a while.

In my dreams, I saw my family standing with the Goddess, looking at a cylinder floating between them like a table with no legs.

"What are you looking at?" I asked as I walked up to them. A misty cloud seemed to surround us all.

My mom looked at me with a big smile. Her eyes were happy to see me.

"Darah, you're here. I am so glad to see you, dear."

My Dad pulled me into a big bear hug. I couldn't help the tears that rimmed my eyes. I missed them all so much. I was grateful to be able to visit like this, even if it was only in my dreams. This was more than I could hope for, and I cherished it.

"I like your hot new friend." My Brother Jason said as he took his turn hugging me.

"It's so good to see you, dork," I said as he stepped away from hugging me.

"I miss you too, big sis." Jason looked amazingly. He was a handsome young man and somehow buffer than he was in real life on Earth.

"Hello, Darah." The Goddess Harmony greeted me with her ethereal smile. Everyone, including myself, was dressed in white. We all seemed to resemble the cloud of mist that surrounded us.

"Hello, Goddess Harmony. Thank you for allowing me to visit my family."

I was so unbelievably blessed. No words will ever convey my gratitude for everything Harmony has gifted me.

"No need to fuss over such a simple thing. Besides, I genuinely enjoy your family. We are fast friends." My family looked at me as the Goddess spoke.

"Part of being in the realm of the Gods means my close friendship with the people of the planets has been hindered, and my suppressed powers limit me from using visions for communication. I need assistance from other gods to appear as a hologram, and gods are usually busy." Harmony said somberly.

"I miss the ability to hang out and fellowship among friends. Having your family here is not typical, but my father, the great creator, allowed this special exception just for me." The Goddess smiled, and my knees felt like they would buckle from her attention's impact on me.

"It works for your family, too, because they like to be able to check on you. My father allowed me to take you from Earth. Now I can have you assist me in saving the Hecat universe from the Kanenites."

The Goddess Harmony smiled sweetly as she looked at each of us.

"Yes, we are tickled pink to be able to check on you, Darling." My Dad said as he smiled brightly at me.

"Here, check this out. We can zoom in on anything. It is wild." Jason insisted I look at the floating disk table thing.

I walked up next to my brother, who was staring at the display that showed Flame organizing my ship and assigning crew duties—doing final inventory checks.

"She is super-hot for an alien chick," Jason said.

"Some things never change," I said as I elbowed him playfully.

"Yeah, Yeah, but it turns out you seem to be batting for both teams now, as you think she is hot too," Jason said, wagging his brow at me, teasing me.

I felt heat flush my cheeks. "How much do you guys see?" I asked.

"We respect your intimate private moments and stay clear from seeing things we know you would be uncomfortable with. I like Terrek. He truly loves you, and I am thrilled you can finally be happy." My mom beamed at me with pride.

I looked at the Goddess Harmony. "Explain why I feel things for Flame when I know I love Terrek?" I asked, wanting to get to the root of things.

Hecat appeared out of nowhere and laughed, "Yes, love, do explain." Where did he come from? I thought, startled.

He stood taller, towering over Harmony as he grabbed her hand and pulled her close, lifting her to his lips. Harmony rolled her eyes at Hecat.

This god's presence and power hit me like a punch of energy. It was hard for me to look upon them. His pale skin glowed bright enough to mute out the definitions of his muscles and features. I hit my knees and covered my eyes.

"Hecat, you're too much! Please beware of your power." Harmony chided.

"Of course, my love, my apologies. I just wanted to pop

over and give you a quick kiss before I continue with my duties."

His powerful presence somehow diminished enough that I could stand up and clearly saw the couple before me. Hecat was handsome, and every inch of him was muscles, mite, and strength.

His long blonde hair was pulled up into a braid. He only wore a leather kilt elaborately woven and stitched to look like armor attire. Somehow, this God was incredibly intimidating, even with his kilt. He turned and stared at me. I almost sank to my knees again when his glowing blue eyes met mine.

"Thank you Darah for helping my Harmony save my universe, I am working on correcting wrongs as well. I need to get back to my duties now. I am honored to have you a part of our universe. I will favor you and your family for all time."

With a charming smile, Hecat disappeared before my eyes. The lingering power that held me captivated dispersed. I took a deep breath and focused on Harmony.

"He can really be too much, but he is working on it. He doesn't usually interact with the beings of his creation. However, he is trying because he knows it is important to me." Harmony reassured me.

"I am speechless but looking forward to knowing you both. I am honored by the blessing." I said, humbled.

"Shall we continue now?" Harmony asked.

Hecat suddenly returned and stood near Harmony, this time his presence was not overpowering me.

"Yes, Please, Goddess." I was eager to understand.

"Darah, my mother is the Goddess of love and is responsible for true mates, soulmates, divine fated mates. I dare not say her name. My mother is as strong as my father. Some say she may be even more powerful. "In a hushed tone, she continued.

"I will not speak my father's name, saying their names are too risky. All Gods covet the power of their name. Being their daughter is also a secret that few know.

My mom has a sense of humor, but the one law that binds

us all is her mating decree. She pairs souls together, and there is no breaking that design." Harmony was speaking as she playfully said.

"Believe me, I had tried to alter my mother's decree when it came to me. But alas, mother does know best." Harmony leaned into Hecat and gave him a gentle kiss.

"The Gods can create chaos when they mess with things they shouldn't," Harmony said sternly, looking at Hecat.

"For example, on the planet of my creation, many people died when a queen was killed because of the antic of that God." Harmony wiggled her pointer finger at Hecat accusingly.

I have forgiven him, but my heart hasn't healed wholly over all my losses. My mother had designed those souls who died on my planet to be paired with their true mates. This caused devastation on my planet. The living lost hope, and the population was doomed to become extinct after the death of so many." I noticed an expression of shame cross over Hecat's features.

"If an un-mated pair were separated by death before they meet and cannot claim each other. My mother will create another mate for the surviving half of the soul. The Goddess of Love could not create mates for the survivors on my planet, so my father and mother worked together to create true mates that my planet could use."

Now, my planet has true mates that will eventually become reincarnated, and when they bond in future lifetimes, they will bond in groups when they choose to return together. Eventually, in future reincarnation, they will all unite and become mates."

"I think I am more confused now," I said, staring at Flame through the disk, trying to understand the butterflies in my chest.

"My dear Darah, you have more than one soul as your divine mate. Flame and Terrek were destined to be together in Hecat's universe. Time is a concept that is different between worlds and the universe and especially between God's realms and the planets.

When you were born, my mother saw that I would choose you. She saw the mess Hecat made of my world. She made Flame and Terrek, your destined mate. You each carry a sliver of each other's soul, and after meeting one another, you recognize your bond and become mated." Harmony's lips grew in a tight line.

"I am still angry at my mother for not warning me of Hecat and his ultimate damage to my world."

Hecat pulled Harmony in for a hug. "I am forever sorry I hurt you. I will spend eternity making it right." He pleaded with Harmony.

"Wait, what did you just say?" I snapped at Harmony in shock.

"Don't worry, dear. It's a good match. My mother does not fail with her mating selections." Harmony said, not looking at me as she stared lovingly into Hecat's eyes.

"Flame is an impressive gal. I am happy you have two strong partners to help keep my baby girl safe, happy, and loved." My Dad said.

"Agreed, they both have gumption enough to be your partners. I am eager to see what color eyes my future grandbabies will have: red, black, or blue?" My mom chimed in, staring at my dad conspiratorially.

"Grandbabies?" this is all too crazy, and somehow, my future love life overwhelmed me.

I felt anxiety rise. My chest tightened, and my palms sweated. The pounding of my heart thrummed in my ears. I saw Terrek in my mind, and I was certain I love him. I looked at the display disk and watched Flame as she worked.

I was attracted to her, and she sent heated vibrations of lust throughout my body. I really liked her and our budding friendship. I just never envisioned falling in love with two people simultaneously. When I think about Flame, Terrek, and

I all together, desire enveloped me, and I wanted that. I craved it. I would not let cravings hurt Terrek, though.

"I love Terrek, and I don't want to complicate that. I already chose Terrek. I consider us married already, for Christ's sake!" I insisted.

I'm trying to ignore my building need for Flame.

"Yes, Terrek is your mate. You love him. He will continue to love you as he will love Flame. Loving Flame doesn't jeopardize what you have with Terrek." Harmony said.

"Can't I wait for another life if we need to, if it's too much for me right now," I said, trying to figure out a way not to complicate life more than it already was?

"Sweety, no, only if one of you should die before you bond. You will always find each other. There is no way around my mother's decree. You will be happy when you accept it. Besides, I know you truly want Flame. It is just a matter of acceptance." Hecat and Harmony shared a look.

I was so upset with Hecat. It took me time to get to know and forgive him so that I could become agreeable. I truly love him now." Hecat kissed Harmony's head and hugged her.

"The three of us together, is this accepted? Will we be judged?" I asked all of them.

"Oh, I see, you did grow up in East Texas, the bible belt of judging people," Jason said with a giggle.

"Darah, you know better than to worry about what others think." My mother scolded me.

"I raised you better than that." She continued.

"Darah, all we care about is your love and happiness. However, that looks and works for you. If my baby girl is happy, then I am happy." My Dad insisted.

"Things are different than the way they are on Earth. It is not uncommon to have polyamorous relationships with multiple partners, whether my mom has designed that or not. Don't worry. Trust how you feel in your heart." Harmony said reassuringly.

"Baby girl, I am so proud of you. Look at how you rallied

the galactic empire and your saving slaves. You deserve love and happiness, and I am honored to watch over you and see how you live an extraordinary life." My Dad said, a bit choked up.

"You're going to make me cry, Daddy. I don't feel extraordinary. I do what is right."

"Darah, honey, you just keep on doing that, and know we love you, and we are always near." My mom said, hugging me.

"Big sis, you know I got your back. Kick ass and take names." Jason's words faded as I woke up and lost my vision of them.

—Ember—

(On planet Harmony,
a universe far away)

I emerged from the seas with my bag full of pearls. Rina, the water dweller, gifted them for my aunt Brooke's baby shower. My mom has me flying all over the place to gather all the gifts and supplies. My auntie helped my mother raise my siblings and I. That means Brooke being pregnant is the event of the century, and my mom was over the moon about it; everything has to be perfect.

Auntie Brooke and Uncle Fang adopted Phoenix when he was orphaned during the war against the vampire a thousand years or so ago. We have been grown for over a century now. Now that Brooke and Fang are expecting, the entire Dragoon Kingdom is celebrating. My mom was so happy.

She was insisting on throwing a surprise baby shower, one of her and Auntie Brooke's customs from their birth world, Earth. I guess that makes me half-human, but I have never been to Earth. Our god portal is one way only. We call it Harmony's delivery door, a nickname my mom and Auntie Brooke named it when they first arrived on this planet through that portal door.

I transformed into my dragon form and flew. Soaring to the grand hall so I can treat myself to the human food that the food replicator delivers through the god portal. I saw my sister Blaze perched on a crystal pedestal cloud that was floating up in our colorful skies.

"Mom is waiting on those pearls. She wishes to hand them

to the jeweler so he can create those necklaces for Auntie." Blaze's voice booms inside my mind.

I landed on the crystal and stared down at the mountain that Harmony's hall was built into.

"I know, Blaze; I was just visiting with the water dwellers; here, take my bag of pearls to Mom." I gently unclenched my claw and dropped the precious jewels into my sister's open claw.

I am craving an animal-style cheeseburger."

Blaze gave me her knowing look as she closed her claw around the bag.

"You better hurry. Mom expects all of us to be there on time." Blaze narrowed her purple slit dragon eye on my Bow and Quiver that Uncle Fang hand carved and made for me. I had it secured to my neck.

"Don't Think about target practice. You will forget about being on time if you decide to shoot those bows." Blazed warned, knowing me too well.

"I promise, just a cheeseburger, and I'll be right there on time." I insisted.

"Papa Stan is making a feast, and you insist on the cheese-burger, okay sister, I'll see you soon." Blaze flew off, laughing at me.

I rolled my eyes and dove off the crystal cloud, heading for the hall. I turned into my skin form and walked into the grand hall. It was sparse because of the surprise celebration. My mother was using all the treasures of the kingdom for the decor of my auntie's baby shower party. She really loves sparklies.

The true mates stopped appearing many years ago once Balance was restored here. The greeters that once stayed at the manor just outside this hall would take shifts to help the newly arriving females adjust well and receive a good support system.

The portal was used to bring us true mates to balance our

planet's population. This world is magic and symbiotic with every magical living thing.

When the Vampire decimated our planet's population and caused much harm, the goddess Harmony created this portal and brought my mom and her sister here from Earth. They saved this world and welcomed all the other true mates.

It was a happy side effect that we could use the enchanted pages of the magic book to order Earth food. Granted, it's replicated, but still a treat, my favorite snack. The portal door was the only one we have on this planet. I had to sneak away here whenever I have the opportunity to get this treat.

I picked up the enchanted book and stared at the blue god portal door. I wrote my order on the blank page and knocked three times. The crystal lights above flashed and chimed, making my nerves flair a warning at me.

When the blue door opened and revealed the blackness of the other side, I was captured. Instead of receiving my food. I was sucked into the door.

This had never happened before. We only received beings through the door. My mother was going to be so mad at me. I didn't even get my cheeseburger. I wondered where in the stars I would end up.

CHAPTER 17

Darah

I sat up slowly, waking from my vision. I could not stop the tears as I noticed that Terrek was already gone. Today, the agenda was to take off. Terrek really should have woken me up, too.

I was glad he didn't because I cherished my family visits. Shaking off my emotions, I jumped in the shower.

Terrek fed Candy, had breakfast, and had my tea ready when I entered the chow.

I love this man so much. He was so attuned to my needs that he ensured I had what I needed. The little things he did were big things to my heart. I drank my tea as I thought of Terrek and Flame.

The potential of us in a relationship together. I was gazing at the leaves in my cup when Flame came in with several new crew members. She looked exhausted.

I saw three hearts in my leaves for my future, and for my present, a dragon appeared. Confused at the vagueness of a dragon, I wondered if it had something to do with the upcoming battle.

I set my cup down when Candy nudged my elbow, wanting me to pet him. I focused on Terrek and Flame as Candy's purring soothed me.

Terrek went to Flame and insisted she sit and eat. Flame sank into the seat next to me. Terrek gave her a plate of food and tea.

"If I sit too long, I will fall asleep right here." Flame said with a yawn.

Flame pulled out a fabric bag from a case she carried. I made sure to get you this tea before we took off." She handed me the dark bag. I smelled the aroma first as excitement hit me. I opened the bag of dried tea leaves that smelled soothing, a sweet and floral scent filled my nose.

"Oh, my goodness, I think I love you!" I said without thought.

"Thank you so much." I tried to side-hug her as she sat next to me.

"What's not to love? I tried to be here before your morning tea but was held up." Flirted Flame.

"It's my favorite flavor. I hope you like it." Flame said. I saw the dark circles under her eyes.

"It smells delicious I can't wait to try some. That's it. You have overdone it. You need sleep, Flame. If your brain is fried from being too tired, you won't be good to anyone." I insisted.

"I know. Things came up last night, and I needed to address it before we left. As soon as we launch, I will get some sleep."

"What are we waiting for? Let's launch now." Terrek said sternly. He looked concerned for Flame.

Flame's lip curled into an amused smile. "I am too tired to argue." I set my cup down when Candy nudged my elbow, wanting me to pet him. I focused on Terrek and Flame as Candy's purring soothed me.

Terrek went to Flame and insisted she sit and eat. Flame

sank into the seat next to me. Terrek gave her a plate of food and tea.

"If I sit too long, I will fall asleep right here." Flame said with a yawn.

Flame pulled out a fabric bag from a case she carried. I made sure to get you this tea before we took off." She handed me the dark bag. I smelled the aroma first as excitement hit me. I opened the bag of dried tea leaves that smelled soothing. The aroma of sweet and floral hit my nose.

"Oh, my goodness, I think I love you!" I said without thought.

"Thank you so much." I tried to side-hug her as she sat next to me.

"What's not to love? I tried to be here before your morning tea but was held up." Flirted Flame.

"It's my favorite flavor. I hope you like it." Flame said. I saw the dark circles under her eyes.

"It smells delicious and I can't wait to try it. That's it. You have overdone it. You need sleep, Flame. If your brain is fried from being too tired, you won't be good to anyone." I insisted.

"I know. Things came up last night, and I needed to address it before we left. As soon as we launch, I will get some sleep."

"What are we waiting for? Let's launch now." Terrek said sternly. He looked concerned for Flame.

Flame's lip curled into an amused smile. "I am too tired to argue."

We left our food and went to the command center. Flame announced the launching countdown for the fleet, and our ship took the lead.

Just like that, our mission started. We were off.

"Now you need to sleep." I grabbed Flame's hand and walked her to my cabin.

My fingers intertwined with her soft, long fingers. I love how the softness of touching her felt. Flame squeezed my hand, and butterflies took off. Even though Flame was clearly exhausted, she walked confidently, and her energy was formidable. I loved how she held my hand and walked past onlookers proudly, displaying our moment of closeness.

"I can sleep in the crew quarters." Flame said in her sleepy voice.

"Stop; you need a comfortable place to sleep with no disturbances." I insist.

I guided her to my room. I wanted to have Flame lay in our bed. The thought of her sleeping in my bedding made me feel close to her.

Flame laid down on our bed. Her formidable presence evaporated the moment the door slid shut. She gave me a grateful look and lifted her hand to cup my face. Flame was vulnerable and looked so worn out.

I removed her boots and covered her. "I love the scent of both of you." I heard Flame mutter as she fell asleep the moment her head hit the pillow.

I released her red hair from its tight bun. She looked so beautiful sleeping. Something about her hair fanned out over my pillow and seeing her in my bed made my belly flutter more.

"Sweet dreams, beautiful lady," I whispered to her before I left my cabin. I had to resist the urge to crawl into bed and snuggle her.

Terrek and Candy met me in the hall. "That is one stubborn Female. Did you get her to sleep?" Terrek asked.

"Yes, she looks like she belongs in our bed," I said.

Terrek chuckled, "I think you may be correct, my love. Flame is special to us."

CHAPTER 18

Darah

"She was so impressive, strong, and beautiful, prettier than a peach. I am attractive to her, Terrek," I said. I was worried I'd upset him.

My little Earthling, have you finally discovered that Flame is our bonded mate? I have been meaning to discuss this with you, but we have been so busy that you seemed unaware. I wanted to give you time to adjust and accept Flame. let nature take its course. I am thrilled you are attracted to Flame. it is to be expected. I am very attracted to her myself.

Tarek kissed me deeply before two crew members came up to us and requested that we get to know the crew members we hadn't met yet.

I looked at Candy closely to see how he reacted to each new person we chatted with. So far, so good; he seemed calm and not too interested.

"That's my good, sweet boy." I cooed as I petted and played with Candy.

I was shocked when just four hours had passed, and Flame was up and looking refreshed and pristine in her uniform.

"No way you got enough rest," I said, aggravated that Flame was pushing herself too much.

"I don't need as much sleep as you, human." Flame said with sass, her smiling red eyes winking at me.

"I wish you would rest better; I feel you are overdoing it. Work smarter, not harder." I said with my own angst and winked back at her stubborn ass.

"Hard work is smart work, Darah." Flame said as we walked to the command center of the ship.

"I am excited to meet up with the Frio engineers, they arrived shortly after Empress Zion requested them to be stationed at Laverian. They saved me years ago after I sustained my spinal injury during an explosion. I had lost honorable soldiers and friends that day. I need my Frio friend to inspect my implants before we enter a fight."

"A spinal injury! I am so sorry that happened to you. I had not realized it was that severe of an injury." Flame was remarkable. I needed to make sure she didn't overwork herself. Flame seems wholly devoted to her duty and is constantly working.

"Are you sure you're feeling ok, hun? I think you should sleep some more, to be sure." I insisted.

"Don't be silly. I am fine, I don't usually bring up my injury but you and Terrek need to know more about me." Flame insisted as she put the viewfinder on.

Laverian appeared, only this view showed a workforce of ships and spacewalkers building a grid like the one around Gia.

"Wow! They work fast." I said in awe at the sight of Laverian with a defense grid nearly wholly built.

"Oh Terrek, your planet is breathtaking!" Flame insisted as she zoomed in on the planet itself.

The deep greens were framed by white clouds. The deep blue and purples of the ocean's surface made a globe of beauty. The three moons, two with rings and one with the weather of ice and clouds, hovered like a sentinel around the giant planet of Laverian.

"Hailing Stealth Davis, Stealth Davis, Stealth Davis, this is Galactic Frio outpost command on empire channel three. Over." Said the monotone voice over the viewing screen.

"Scans verify the DNA lifeforce of the Frio Command to verify that the caller was genuine, Identity accepted." The computer-upgraded AI announced.

"Galactic Frio, this is Stealth Davis, code three accepted switch to hologram Gia's Commander Flame. Over." Flame responded regally.

"Stealth Davis, switching to hologram channel now, Galactic Frio, out." The monotone voice droned.

Seconds later, Flame's hologram initiated on her wrist. The face of a grey spaceman with big grey lizard-like eyes appeared. Its features were not very distinctive. big eyes, a flat nose, and a small mouth reminded me of the little green men depicted on Earth, something I imagined from Area 51. I suppressed a giggle thinking about the comparison.

"Glacier, it is so good of you to be here in person. I truly value your support and speediest work." Flame greeted the grey man affectionately.

"I could not pass up the opportunity to see my favorite fire." The monotone man said with no expression to match his affection for Flame.

"I am happy to be able to see you, my friend. I am five hours out. I brought you blue ice stones from the north quadrant. Looking forward to giving you a warm hug." Flame laughed.

"Keep your fires clear from me, you kinetic Female. I will, however, be very grateful for the blue ice stones; you spoil me, truly." The monotone voice was odd, not matching the playful words he spoke, and with the bland facial expression of the Frio spaceman, I was officially intrigued.

"I knew you would, so I grabbed them up when I had the opportunity. I will prepare the infirmary med center and lower our ship's temperature. See you in a few hours." Flame had a softness about her when she spoke to the Frio man.

Their transmission ended, and Flame ran scans and gave orders to the crew. I silently hovered, staying out of her way. I shadowed her as we entered the med center. I finally had to ask.

"What do you need the med center for?" Flame looked at me. She seemed a bit shy. Seriously, Flame was shy; she was always so confident. I was even more curious.

"You don't have to tell me if you're uncomfortable." I offered, not wanting to be pushy.

Terrek came to us with Candy in tow. "I was busy with some of the crew learning the engineering of the space jump engine. Time got away from me, but I wanted to ensure you two are well." He Said has he handed Flame and me a bottle of water.

My pink water bottle and a Galactic Empire force bottle for Flame.

"I love you. Thank you for taking care of us." I gave Terrek a sweet kiss. Candy rubbed against my thigh. Then he rubbed against Flame's thigh.

Flame took a long drink of her water. Is it weird that I thought she was sexy at that moment?

"Thank you. I needed that, Terrek." Flame said.

"I need my implants charged before we fight." Flame showed us her golden metallic Tattoos.

"I want to prepare you both. I am . . . Uh . . . I am not the same when I am in a battle." Flame tried to explain.

We entered the infirmary and left Candy to guard the outside of the door.

"I have Nanos, Frio technology implanted like added veins that feed my strength. The Nanos will slowly burn out over time and use. I must recharge them so I can fight to the best of my ability.

I sensed her insecurity flair up as I looked into her vulnerable eyes. I was instantly concerned.

"I don't care what you are when you fight as long as you come back safe and whole," I said, trying to support Flame. The last thing she needed was to worry about me judging her.

"I am not sure I can put it into words. I think I need to demonstrate for you to understand. I want to show you. I think you should brace yourselves.

CHAPTER 19

Darah

Flame began to undress. My heart sped up. I looked at Terrek. He gave me an excited look and nodded, letting me know he was good. My eyes drew in on Flame's long fingers as she unzipped her uniform.

As Flame exposed her skin inch by inch, I felt heat flush my cheeks, and goosebumps spread up my arms. My core was heating up. She exposed those golden metallic markings that only turned me on more.

I took a breath, trying to be rational about this. Flame was trying to communicate something important, and I needed to focus on her, and not be a horny creep about it.

"I am deadly in a fight, not just because I am a seasoned warrior, but because I have the advantage of my species and the Frio implants. I am the only Fire blood that has these implants."

Flame stood before us in black panties, looking like a goddess. She had a golden metallic design on her skin like a sexy tattoo in a corset around her ribs, weaving over her shoulders and around her breast around her thighs, down her long legs, from her upper arms to her toes, a beautiful liquid golden weave that moved like metallic lava.

"So, fucking sexy." I exhaled.

Flame's eyes went molten with heat as she looked at me. She shook it off to continue her speech.

"I can walk and fight because my friend Glacier specifically engineered these implants. These are organic nanomachines. They infused into my body. My fire blood mutated with the Nanos, allowing me to express fire from my fingernails when I take battle form.

I wanted you to see all of me. My species frowns on my markings, and it is a controversy. More than ever before, I have to prove my position and worthiness as a warrior to keep my rank and station in the galactic empire.

I know you two are my bond mates. I want you both to know the stigma I carry with my implants. I must be honest and up front." Flame's red eyes shadowed over with insecurity.

"My Fire blood species can morph into a battle form. We can use our venom and fire in a fight. My nanos enhance those natural abilities.

Flame took a deep breath as she suddenly shifted before my eyes. Her features grew fierce, morphing just enough to become scary-looking.

She resembled an actual demon with her red eyes, and she hissed out her snake-like fangs and presented them to us. Her nails looked like wicked black claws, and sharp smoke whirled out from them. She looked like she had grown a foot or two taller. I remembered when Empress Zion transformed similarly at the declaration of war vote.

I gasped with fear at the sight of Flame so close and terrifying. I had stepped back into Terrek's chest. He rubbed my upper arms, soothing me.

"She is exceptional. Look at how amazing she is?" Terrek cooed in my ear.

I evaluated this scary version of Flame. Her golden lines

looked like lava moving like a river around her body. Her features were harsh now, and those eyes and fangs were very intimidating. Her skin turned a shade of red. Flame stood in front of us on display, allowing us to watch her. She must have been fearless to do this. Once I got past the initial shock, I watched her. She was still so beautiful to me.

Flame's eyes found reassurance when she locked her gaze on Terrek. Then she lowered her eyes to look into mine. When I relaxed and gave her a soft smile, Flame let her battle form fade into her usual beautiful self.

"Remind me never to piss you off," I said with a smile.

"You are amazing. Terrek is right. You are exceptional." Flame gave me a sexy grin.

Standing before us on full display with just a pair of black panties, my heart pounded as I reacted to her beauty. Her sultry eyes met mine with hunger, and I reached up to cup her cheeks and pulled her down to my lips for a soft, seductive kiss.

The moment I tasted her, my body reacted with need. I was wrapped up in her arms. Her skin was silky and feverish. The world just disappeared, and she was wholly what I needed at that moment.

The AI announcement blared, interrupting our embrace as Flame reluctantly pulled away to respond. Her sexy breasts heaved, and her nipples pebbled hard. It was all I had to resist latching my mouth onto her inviting, perky nipples.

I want to map out her golden lines with my mouth and kiss every inch of her. I felt Terrek embrace me from behind. He leaned in and nibbled my ear.

"I don't blame you, Darah. She is a sweet burn indeed." I moaned and arched my ass into his groin.

He slowly unzipped my uniform and let it fall to the floor. Flame ended her response to the AI, authoring a reboot on some routine system update.

"These computers always have the worst timing." Flame said.

Forgetting the disruption, Flame focused her hungry attention on me. I felt my body drench my panties with need. My throbbing clit demanded attention. Terrek inhaled deeply, releasing a moan.

"Mmm, you both smell ready with arousal."

Flame stepped up to help Terrek remove my bra. As my breasts bounced, she gripped them in her soft hands and stared into my eyes.

"If you are truly ready, there is no going back. I have been restraining myself. I know I will claim you both if we continue." Flame warned as a last attempt to give me more time if needed.

I realized then that I had been resisting myself for too long. At that moment, all I knew was that I wanted and needed her just as much as I craved Terrek.

"Please." I sighed.

Flame leaned over my shoulder and kissed Terrek. I was sandwiched between them. I looked up and saw them passionately kissing. This was so fucking hot.

They looked hot together. I was not jealous. I wanted to see more of them being intimate. Nope, no more resisting. I wanted this to be my life. I grabbed Flame's nipple with my mouth. The sensation of her soft sexiness and Terrek's hardness surrounding me was like a euphoric cocoon.

I heard Flame moan as she broke away from kissing Terrek to cup my head as I played with her beautiful breast. They were smaller than my own, her perky breast were perfect with her redden nipples harden ready for my mouth. I felt Terrek move back and heard him unzip his uniform. Flame walked me backward to the exam bed.

I reluctantly released my mouth from her decadent nipple. I took the hint and laid back on the bed. Flame removed my panties and stared at me, taking every detail in. When her eyes locked on mine, she asked in a sultry voice.

"I need to hear you tell me you are ready and willing to bond."

"Yes, Flame, I want you and all of this, Terrek, you and me from now on," I vowed my certainty. I know I had barely accepted all this, but something in my soul had me taking the leap of love for both of them.

Flame leaned down to kiss me, her hands in my hair.

"I was hoping you'd say yes." She purred into my ear as she kissed my neck, sending gooseflesh down my arms.

"Mmm, oh, you feel so damn good." I encouraged them as her hands kneaded and caressed my body.

Flame worked her mouth and hands down my body, I spread my legs and unraveled her bun to hold her hair back as she used her mouth to devour my pussy.

Terrek kissed my mouth, and then he worked on my breast. I was engulfed in a whirl of sensations with his hands and mouth and her hands and mouth all at once.

Flame worked magic on my core, her softness in contrast to Terrek's hardness had me feeling bliss in a completely new experience. My lover's balance made me feel complete and washed in perfect bliss.

Terrek moved away from us and watched, stroking his hard cock as Flame and I had our moment together. I gazed down when Flame released her latch on my clit with a sexy wet pop.

"You taste like ambrosia." Flame said as she consumed me with her loving gaze. She returned to feasting on me. Her rhythm and pressure were perfect, and her mouth and tongue heated up in temperature. The heat along with her vibrating tongue was out of this world fantastic.

Sparkles of magic light erupted everywhere she made contact with my skin. I felt my core sending bolts of exotic sensations throughout my body. My orgasm was built, and then I erupted.

"MMMM, I am cumming!" I moaned as Flame worked her finger inside me and twirled her tongue perfectly around my clit.

"Flame released me with a satisfied smile. My wetness marked her sexy lips.

"That's a good girl." Flame praised me.

"You're a good girl." Terrek pulled Flame up to kiss her deeply. Moaning a sexy growl when Flame grabbed his thick pulsing cock. That magic light was hypnotic as they touched and kissed each other.

"I'll show you I can be a bad girl too." Flame said as she broke away from his kiss and went to her knees to take him into her mouth.

"Just like that, you suck that cock so well, MMMM." Terrek moaned, letting his head fall back, just getting lost in the ecstasy of Flame's mouth.

"You are perfectly big." Flame panted as she took a breath to continue working her magic on Terrek.

I sat up on my elbows, basking in the aftermath of my orgasm and getting worked up again, watching Terrek and Flame have this sexy moment. It was a magical sight. Everything felt so perfect.

"You keep that up. I will explode into that sexy mouth of yours, Flame." Terrek warned.

She let go of his cock with a pop, and he lifted her by her ass so he could kiss her and slide his big cock into her pussy.

The moan they both let out at his entry had me placing my fingers into myself—Terrek and Flame were lost in one another as they bonded.

The sight of him fucking her while standing was sexy as hell. He was so strong, and Flame's body softened as she submitted. She was so feminine and lost in lust in his arms. Her sexy dark red hair fell down her back in waves as she leaned back, grinding into Terrek, keeping the frantic pace he set.

Flame hit her orgasm and let out a sexy cry of release. Her fangs extended as she moved forward and bit down on his neck.

"Fuck! MMM," Terrek growled as he came into Flame, losing it when she bit him.

They stood there while the bonding took hold. The light embraced them both like a cloak. Terrek was holding Flame to him, and Flame latched onto his neck. Moments passed before Flame lifted her head and stared lovingly into Terrek's black eyes.

Love was clearly in their gazes. This was a special moment for them. My heart melted to be able to witness it. Terrek Kissed Flame as she unwrapped her legs and stood still, hugging and kissing her new mate.

I wanted to congratulate them as I felt so happy, but I did not want to ruin the moment.

"You big Laverian male, you sure know how to rock a woman's world." Flame said teasingly.

"You, my sweet Fire, are the one who can set fire to my world." Terrek countered.

Flame and Terrek turned, looked at me, and reached for me. As Terrek cupped my face, pulling me close to them. I kissed Terrek and then Flame, tasting all of us together.

"Well, if you ask me, you two knock my world off its axis," I said as my two lovers held me in our aftermath.

"Is that so?" Flame said as she approached me. Her cheek flushed after cumming.

"Yes, definitely yes!" I crooned as I had both their attention now. I slid off the bed and patted it as an invitation for Flame to take my spot.

Flame laid back on the exam table and spread her long legs, her bare lips revealing her sexy pussy and swollen clit. My mouth watered, wanting to taste her and Terrek together.

I leaned down and latched onto her sweet wet Clit. She grabbed my hair and ground into me as I ate her up. The mix of her sweet flavor mixed with him was arousing.

I felt her pussy walls clamp around my fingers as she came for me too. The feeling was empowering to be able to satisfy her. Terrek entered me from behind, and the bonding light grew brighter.

It was the best moment of my life when all three of us came together.

I crawled up on top of her, and we softly kissed as I lay next to her. I felt Terrek using his hands and fingers to work both Flame and me as we made out, our breasts smashed together, her hands in my hair, mine all over her.

Our hips grinding as Terrek finger fucked us. We came at the same time again when Flame bit down on my neck. I felt her hot venom enter my veins, and my body grew high, and all my sensations heightened. My responding orgasm was intense and out of this world good.

I bit down on hers when she released my neck, bonding us completely. I leaned up and gazed down at her sexy red eyes. Her hair splayed out like a halo, and her cheeks flushed red. Her breast heaving showcasing her pert tight red nipples. She was the sexiest Female I had ever seen, and she was mine now. She was ours. This was amazing. The light faded away, and without a doubt, I knew I'd have both my mates for the rest of my life.

I leaned down and kissed her sweetly. Terrek helped me off the exam bed. He kissed me sweetly and helped Flame stand. He pulled Flame into us. We took turns kissing and being together for the first time as a triad.

The AI announcement once again disturbed our perfect moment.

"Approaching the ship, the Frio commander, Glacier, requests access to enter our docking port."

"I guess that means we need to get dressed." I pouted.

Reluctantly, we all separated and did a quick cleanup before we dressed to welcome our guests.

"Do your legs feel like Jello to you too?" I asked Flame as we pulled our pants on.

"Lover, my whole body feels delicious with a sweet reminder of how you both claimed me." Flame's flirty voice stirred my senses again.

… _Flame_ …

"My mother, being Empress Zion, has always had an unfounded reputation of granting me favoritism. The controversy of my fighting after my injury. I fight every day to be the best of the best and to prove them all wrong.

Most of those who work with me and my mother know better, but those who are sticklers of traditions have a critical opinion of me. I have to be vigilant with my duties. Or I would find a way to delegate and spend our bonding day alone, just the three of us."

"Fuck those assholes!" Darah said, angry for me. My tiny feisty Earthling.

"Once my injury occurred, I was expected to comply with retirement procedures. I just wasn't ready to accept that my fighting days were done. I commissioned Emperor Glacier to make these implants to help me have the fighting edge."

"My fierce, brave warrior woman," Terrek said as he grabbed my hand.

"We did this during my leave as I appealed my retirement. It was risky, and we both knew the consequences if it failed. Glacier did not hesitate to help me. I once saved his space city from an attack that would have destroyed his city and family."

"He sounds like a great friend, Flame," Darah mentioned.

"He is a great being. The Frio can't take heat. I am naturally hot with my fire blood. He developed a special suit to keep him cold as he worked on me. This invention enabled his kind to work with all the Galactic Empires.

Glacier is a genius. I am lucky to call him my friend. He saved my career and continues to provide defensive technology to our forces."

"Is he leading the workforce building the protection around my planet?" Terrek asked.

"Yes, babe, he is the only one I trust to ensure everything is exceptionally made," I said. Terrek kissed the top of my head.

"I can't thank you enough for protecting my planet," Terrek whispered affectionately.

"The Hellfire Sun in the north Quadrant makes it impossible for the Frio species to travel to that sector. It is too hot for them in that solar environment, even with their suits and solar shields."

Darah squeezed my hand and pulled me closer as we walked the halls.

"The rare blue ice crystals that form on a particular comment go through the north quadrant and are a coveted resource for the Frio people. It helps heal a specific affliction of their species.

When my sources told me Glacier was seeking a blue ice crystal, I made a special mission to track down that comment and collect whatever ice crystal we could manage. We have three, and the comments ice crystals will take time to grow again.

I hope these blue ice crystals can save whomever Glacier needs them for."

"What a great friend you have, Flame. I am eager to meet Glacier," Darah said.

"I am ever grateful to the Frio people and my friend Glacier. I feel confident he will engineer the best defensive grid for Laverian. I am looking forward to kicking some Kanenites ass! I can't stand a tyrant. I hate that the Laverian world has been harvested." I said with emotion.

"You honor my people and I. Flame, I am proud you are one of us now and to have you on my side," Terrek said humbly.

"Remind me never to get on your bad side, Flame. You are badass. You give my lady parts a quiver whenever I look at you." Darah said with her goofiness.

She had no clue that when I looked at her, I get hungry for her. I sucked in a breath as heat flooded my loins again. A long, silent pause had my eyes locked on hers.

Terrek cleared his throat and squeezed my hand. Shaking my head from the lusty haze, I looked at Terrek. Damn, he affected me the same. Both my mates are finally mine.

I knew the moment I saw them that they were mine. I just needed to make sure they were worthy. I saw in Terrek's eyes recognition. When Darah's eyes met mine, I saw the attraction, but somehow, my gut told me she was unfamiliar with the mate bond.

Fighting myself, my burning need to act has been the hardest self-restraint I have ever had to achieve. The Gods saw fit to give me worthy partners. My species values strength.

I have worked my way through the ranks even with the stain of my spinal injury. Gaining respect among my peers was always a challenge. These two emulate strength.

I leaned down and gave Darah a sweet kiss. I was thrilled that I could act on my instinct and urges to do so. As we walked, I pull my hair up to ensure uniform compliance.

"You should leave it down. I like seeing your hair free." Darah suggested.

"It is out of uniform compliance when it is down," I said as I quickly tied my hair up. I winked at her.

"Last I checked, I was captain of this ship, so if you want to wear it down, you can." My sassy girl declared with that sexy southern drawl.

"You are just a naughty rebel." I lightly smacked her curvy ass. I loved that I could freely touch her now. It was so hard to resist my need for her and Terrek.

"I'll show you naughty later," Darah said as we stood outside the docking port airlock. We saw the outside door slide open through the window as the AI allowed Glacier's ship access.

He stepped in wearing his tight suit and had a small space fabric helmet fitted over his head.

The sliding door closed. The temperature dropped through-out the ship to help accommodate the Frio species.

"It's colder than a witch's tit in a brass bra." Darah said as she rubbed her arms.

"We can stop to get you a jacket on our way back to the infirmary," I suggested.

Terrek pulled Darah into his arms to help keep her warm. The interior door slid open, and Glacier stepped through. He gave me a salute in the way of his kind.

I placed my fist over my heart and bowed in the way of mine and then in the way of his people. I always want to hug this male, but I knew I was too hot to do so comfortably for his Frio body.

"I am so glad to see you, Glacier. I am happy to introduce you to my bond mates.

This Is Darah, and this is Terrek."

"Congratulation . . ." Glacier drones in his monotone voice. I am used to his talking style, but I can see Darah's curi-osity as if she wonders how sincere the Frio Emperor was.

"Thank you, Glacier; I know you are truly happy for me. I am one lucky Female." I said as I escorted Glacier to the exam room.

I entered the room, and the smell of our mingled sex still permeated the air. I don't think I will ever look at an exam bed the same. This room became the most important memory of my life.

I looked at Darah and Terrek as they held hands, silently supporting me while Glacier attached wires and tubes. I smiled warmly at them. I was glad they wanted to support me. I was also sad they will witness my suffering. This is very painful. I must endure it to discharge my liquid fire in a fight and not be depleted.

"You don't have to watch. This is painful, and I don't want to worry either of you," I said, giving them a choice to stay or go.

Glacier pulled a cylinder out, the bright glowing Nanos

flowing endlessly, moving. My lifeline will always be these golden machines. I could feel the heat radiating off the cylinder. Glacier struggled to place the container in the dispensing device.

"Allow me to assist you, Glacier." Terrek's profoundly concerned voice announced as he took the hot Nanos from Glaciers gloved hands.

"Do be diligent when handling the nano containment." Glacier droned in his strange voice.

The feeling of anxiety rolled off him in waves. I could smell Terrek's flesh burn as his finger placed the cylinder into its place.

"You burned your fingers!" I gasped, feeling bad he had hurt himself.

"I am well, my Fire. Don't worry. I can handle a little heat," Terrek said as he stepped back with Darah.

Darah kissed the tips of his fingers, and they both focused on me again.

"Not a chance, Flame. We will not leave your side," Darah said as she tried to look over Terrek's burnt fingertips. He waved his hand like it was no big deal.

I laid back and bit down on the mouthguard Glacier handed me.

"Ready?" Glacier droned.

I took a deep breath and nodded. Pain hit me hard as I growled and bit down. The Nanos were being plunged into my implants and vascular system.

"Can you help her with the pain?" Darah asked with a cry of concern. I felt her grab my hand and rub my forehead.

"She is burning up. Is it safe?" Darah was worried.

"The nano burns out any pain-relieving medicine during this injection procedure. Or I would make sure she felt no pain." My Frio friend tried to explain.

I felt Terrek move to my other side, and he whispered in my ear.

"You are brave and strong, my Fire, you are doing well, and it is almost over."

I was experiencing molten lava melting me from the inside out. This pain was always so excruciating.

I usually have Glacier by my side during this procedure. Now, I had a room with the people who loved and valued me. Somehow, the suffering was easier to have them there to support me.

When the pain subsided, I sat up. Darah held my face cupped in her hands as she looked deeply into my eyes to ensure I was well. I gave her a soft kiss.

"I need to go to my cooling chamber," Glacier said. I know this procedure hurt him as well, being exposed to heat.

"Thank you, friend." I meekly said, still exhausted from the fire in my system.

I moved to get off the exam table when I felt Darah unplugging the device and removing the wires and tubes. Terrek pulled me into his arms, cradling me to his chest. The sound of his heartbeat and the smell of his male scent was so soothing I fell limp in his arms.

This was such a gift, letting my partners take care of me. No one had cared for me like this since I was a child. People think my mother is granting me exceptions. Rather, she demands more of me than most because I am her child. I love her, but she is demanding; after all, she is the Empress.

My mother had asked me if I had found my mates. Her ever-watchful eyes don't miss much. I told her I did, but my Earthling needed time. My mother will be happy I have completed our mate bond. I get the feeling my mother was ready for grandbabies.

I wonder if she will let her softer side show with our future children. Terrek gently laid me down on their bed . . . Our bed now. I felt Darah hold me, spooning me from behind. I was in Love. I felt so undeserving of these two. I fell into a deep recovery sleep.

CHAPTER 20

Darah

"I did not like seeing her suffer in pain like that," I told Terrek as I lay behind Flame, rubbing her head as she slept.

"I know. I did not like her suffering either. She is a brave warrior." Terrek bent down to kiss Flame's brow, then gave me a sweet kiss.

"Stay with her. I need to see about something." Terrek turned and left us.

I wonder what he had brewing. He looked determined. I kissed Flame's neck and fell asleep with her in my arms. This time, there was only darkness, no dreams, and no family visits. I woke up feeling disappointed.

That feeling vanished when Flame turned towards me. Tingles rushed over my body, all giddy for the sexy woman looking at me with love in her red eyes.

"How are you feeling?" I asked with my sleepy voice.

"Better, especially waking up in your arms, beautiful." Flame kissed me sweetly before she got up.

"Why don't we stay in bed all day?" I asked with a pout, patting the bed, hoping she would jump back in.

"I would rather spend all day in bed with you, my sweet Darah. Unfortunately, war waits for no one. We have a lot of people to save."

"You are right. I don't want you to push yourself too hard. You just had a painful procedure."

"Pain I can handle, resisting you and all your sexiness, now that is the true suffering." Flame said as she wrapped her beautiful dark red hair up tight.

"You're the sexy one, you she-devil," I said as I rolled out of bed reluctantly and rushed to use the bathroom.

Flame walked up to me she bent down and kissed me deeply, her tongue tasting fresh from the mouth cleanser in the bathroom.

"Now that's what I call a kiss," I said as she left me hot and breathless. Unlike Terrek's commanding, hard kisses, her kisses were soft and sultry. I am not comparing. I was thrilled I had my yin and yang, the perfect blend.

We stepped out into the hall where Terrek stood with a small group of crew members.

"Oh, good, you're up. I was waiting for you. I did not want to disturb you ladies and your resting time." He leaned down to kiss me.

"Do you feel well, my Flame?" Terrek asked, looking her over to be sure.

"Yes, I feel great." Flame said as she smiled up at him. Terrek leaned in to kiss her sweetly, too.

"Good, just the way I like it. My girls are happy and healthy." Terrek turned to the crew.

"Okay, let's get this job done." He said as they carried tools and materials into our room.

"What are you up to?" I asked curiously.

"I am extending our bed. We need to make room so Flame will feel welcomed."

"Is that not the sweetest damn thing?" I said as I looked

at Flame, who looked like she was holding back tears that brimmed her eyes.

"Oh, Hun, we want you in our bed. You are our mate. It is now your bed, too." I said as I pulled her in for a Texas-sized hug.

Terrek pulled us both into a big hug. "You are ours forever. I go wherever you two go."

He kissed our heads, patted our butts, and then turned to help the crew build a big enough bed for us.

"I don't know why that choked me up. I am just so happy." Flame said as she composed herself, and we went back to duty.

"I think we all deserve our happiness. I am glad I have you, too, Flame." I said as we held hands as we went to the command deck.

The defense grid was almost entirely built. The Frio engineers were spacewalkers working like busy ants efficiently with a determined purpose.

Watching them on the viewing display was fascinating. They were in outer space as if they were on a planet. Free of the protections that we would need. Flame sent a drone with blue ice crystals to deliver to Glacier. He sent a video message in return.

"My favorite Fire, I could never repay you for this gift." The droning voice said, and his almost featureless face still conveyed deep gratitude.

"No need to ever repay me, my friend. I owe you more than those blue ice crystals could ever amount to."

"I would burn in a scorching fire for you, my dear friend Flame," Glacier said with a salute.

I knew that must have been a huge compliment from a Frio being. I reached out for Flame's hand and squeezed hers. I know how he feels. I would die for her, for Terrek, without hesitation.

"That male truly respects you," I said as a censor alarm blared.

The AI announcement called out. "Unknown lifeform is being tracked on Laverian."

"Mark the location and get a jump ship ready." Flame demanded as a commotion erupted among the crew.

"Where did it come from? Do you think it is a Kanenites spy?" I asked, my heart was pounding.

I rushed after Flame as we made our way to the jump pods. Terrek ran up to us just as the door opened.

"I am not sure, but it does not matter. I will find out." Flame said all business.

"I go wherever you two go!" Terrek said as he handed each of us the galaxtic empires modified device wands.

We quickly boarded the jump ship. We were suctioned to our seats like a magnet. As the pod jumped away from Stealth Davis, we flew to the location of the lifeform that appeared out of nowhere on our radar.

"This doesn't make sense. No craft has entered the planet's atmosphere or been in the range of our censors." Flame looked concerned.

"They have only plant life and microbial and the prill fish left on Laverian. There should be no lifeform on the surface." Flame tried to figure out how a lifeform was on the surface, and she did not look happy about not knowing. Her forehead crinkled with stress lines, and her face reddened. She hit scanning buttons with hard jabs.

She flew us to the surface area the beacon was tracking. In our viewing screen stood a tall woman dressed in a blue dress. She carried a bow and quiver full of arrows. Her hair was braided up like I would imagine Vikings did. The female looked confused and stared at our pod in shock.

"Who are you, and where did you come from?" Flame asked through an intercom that projected her demand outside our ship.

The woman stood taller. Her shock was replaced by defiance.

"I am Ember of the Dragoons. I came from the Goddess

Harmony's god portal. Harmony has some explaining to do!" Ember shouted back at us.

I instantly relaxed, "If Harmony sent her, she must be a friend, not a foe." I insisted my intuition telling me so.

"There you go again, being too trusting." Flame said to me with an eye roll.

"I do not recognize her. She has purple slit eyes like the chetaht. She seems like a predator to me." Terrek spoke.

"You two are too much; that girl got here as I did. If Harmony sent her, that's all I needed to vouch for her worthiness," I said, knowing in my gut that Ember was a friend.

"Please, Flame, land this thing so we can talk to her properly. I need to teach you two some southern hospitalities, geez," Darah said.

"Woman! She hasn't been deemed worthy, but I will try to be nice. Only because you asked with that sexy, southern accent." Flame said as she landed our jump pod, and we exited.

The beautiful lady in the blue dress approached us confidently. Terrek stepped in front of Flame and me, taking a defensive stance. I rolled my eyes at Flame, who looked at our big purple male as if to get him to help her convince me to be cautious. Before I had the chance to move, I heard the stranger speak.

"Chill out there, big male. I will not harm you or your females." Ember said.

I stepped next to Terrek. He did not take his suspicious eyes off this lady. Flame stood to his other side. I could feel Terrek tense. He did not speak. Flame looked stern, staring at Ember with a hardness, a visual warning. What a sight we must make.

"I smell the fire in your blood, but you are not a dragon. I smell that you have claimed these two. Your fire marks them. The lady said to Flame.

He smells like he is of this world,» she said, staring at Terrek.

She flared her nostrils toward me.

"You are an earthling. Do any of you know why Harmony has brought me here?" She demanded, not very happy that she was here.

"First off, I am Darah from Texas on earth. Harmony brought me here, too. This big guy is Terrek of this planet. This world is called Laverian. This is Flame; she is from the planet Gia, a warrior world." I introduced my family, trying to break the ice.

"How are you able to smell what we are?" I asked curiously.

"I am Dragoon. My senses are excellent."

"Dragoon?" what does that mean?

"My mother told me that earthlings have heard legends of dragons. Do you not know what a dragon is?"

"I did not know dragons were real. My apologies. How does your mother know about Earth?"

"My mother is from the Earth. The magic of my world changed them into Dragoons. I am half earthling but wholly Dragoon. Dragoon is the family name of our most powerful dragon bloodline."

"You must be deemed worthy." Flame said sharply.

"Can you not smell a lie on me?" Ember asked Flame.

"I cannot smell a lie; can you smell a lie?" Flame retorted. Damn, she was hot when she was in boss mode.

"Curious, I smell your fire; you are somehow related to my dragon. But you are not a dragon."

"Just because we share names related to fire doesn't make us related." Flame said with her flair.

Flame looked at me, leaned behind Terrek's back, and mouthed, "What is a dragon?"

"Will you disarm yourself so we can go back to the ship and discuss this so we can figure everything out together?"

Terrek asked, holding out his hand for her bow and quivers.

"Look, I only wanted some "IN & OUT" out-animal style cheeseburger. That damn blue door opened and sucked me into it. It has never taken any of us before.

It was supposed to be one way, only bringing the people Harmony has chosen to my world. That and the food replicator sends us earth food when we request it." Ember rattled on, seemingly frustrated.

"My family must be worried sick. I want to go home." Ember insisted.

I was taken when I fell into that koi pond, but I had no family left on Earth, so being here was not terrible for me. Ember seems sad that she is here. I felt sorry for her.

"I promise the next vision I have with Harmony. I will ask her about you. If anyone can send you home, it will be her."

Ember took her bow and quiver and reluctantly handed them to Terrek.

"Be careful with this; my Uncle Fang made these for me. He hand-carved my bow and each arrow, even using good wood. The enchanted wood the trees give freely. I will be fire-spitting mad if you damage it."

"Noted; I will take care of your bow," Terrek promised. He seemed a bit more at ease.

"If you are worthy, I will return it to you." Flame said, looking skeptical.

"What magic makes your metal fly?" Ember asked as she stepped into our jump pod.

"Magic? No magic. We use engines. What class level is your planet rated?" Flame asked.

"Class level? I am from planet Harmony. The goddess herself created my world. We fly using our wings, and we never go to space." Ember said simply.

"I never went to space before, and I ended up here going through the god portal myself. We have that in common, but I can teach you. Everything is so fascinating. Maybe you will enjoy your experience traveling in space." I suggested trying to relate to Ember.

"She needs to be deemed worthy before we offer anything to her freely." Flame chided me.

"Whatever! Let's get this over with." Ember said.

We jumped back into space and reattached to Stealth Davis. We escorted Ember to the chair.

"Is this for real? You want me to allow you to strap me down in that chair?"

"It won't hurt you; it is just customary." I insisted.

"Just so you know, I am willingly trying to appease you by sitting in this chair. However, if you try to hurt me, my dragon will protect me. It will destroy this vessel, and I guess that is a quick way to discover if a dragon can survive space."

Ember sat and let me strap her down. I was feeling a bit worried about her turning into a dragon. Was she for real?

Flame turned on the worthy detector. The image showed a dragon flying in a colorful sky; the dragon dodged a crystal platform floating with the clouds. It looks like a beautiful place. The dragons looked terrific. One blew fire playfully. The machine dinged green, declaring Ember worthy.

"That is a dragon," I said to Flame, who was wide-eyed and enthralled at the images displayed.

"A worthy dragon; I wish I could become something that cool." Flame said with respect in her voice.

"Strong women surround me," Terrek said as I unstrapped Ember from the chair.

"We don't have time to figure all this out. We have to leave for our designated rendezvous for the invasion." Flame said, reminding us that we have slaves to save.

"What invasion?" Ember asked, a bit alarmed.

"Laverian was attacked and harvested by these evil guys called the Kanenites. Terrek's people and the beings from other worlds are held prisoners as enslaved people. We have devised a plan of attack to save these people, animals, and resources and return them home."

"I will help you fry some evil asses. My world got rid of our evil vampire. I hoped that would be the last of any evil we ever faced. If I can help you fight, that is the least I can do to repay the Goddess Harmony." Ember offered without hesitation. I like this lady. She will fit right in.

"Welcome to the club," I said. Everyone looked oddly at me; I guess something in the translation was off with my earth slang.

"It just means we are happy to have you join us."

"I am happy to be a part of the club that kills the evil guys," Ember said, and we all laughed.

"I need to return home as soon as possible, so let's go fry some evilness." Ember insisted.

We headed to our destination after we gave Ember a quick tour of Stealth Davis and set her up in a crew bunk.

Talking significantly about saving the enslaved people was good, but suddenly, a hollow in the pit of my stomach weighed me down. I was terrified of Terrek and Flame being injured or killed. I could not lose my family again. I won't survive it.

I looked around the ship. The crew members and the warriors were busy checking all components and preparing the ship for battle. I saw a pallet of medical supplies being inventoried by medics, and reality sank in. Some of these people will be injured or worse. We are just hours away from a very intense battle.

Looking around, I saw that everyone was working and seemingly cool, just excited about the war we were about to engage in. They must be made of badassery, some tough stuff. I both admired and feared for them. I wished that I had it in me to be so cool.

Anxiety suddenly consumed me, my heart pounding, thinking about Flame being injured again. Or Terrek being hurt. They could die. I could not let them get hurt or die. I was helpless to control the unknown outcome. I started to hyperventilate, breathing fast and feeling dizzy with panic. I was fighting not to let it show.

Terrek first sensed it as he stopped helping a crew member and came directly to me. He wrapped me in his arms and carried me to the chow hall. He sat me on the table and got me a hot, fresh cup of tea.

Candy jumped on the table to lay his head on my lap. "Thank you, dear," I said, choked up.

Rubbing Candy's silky ears helps to calm me.

"Darah, don't be scared. I believe we will prevail. How can we not? We have your goddess on our side." Terrek tried to soothe me.

Ember came into the chow hall. Candy jumped down and ran to her. He jumped up to hug her and smell her face. Ember laughed and sank her hands into his soft fur.

"Hello, you sweet beast, I like you furry guy." Ember cooed as she sniffed Candy.

"Well, that's new; I am glad he likes you." I was starting to calm down.

"I smelled your anxiety and wanted to check on you. My Aunt Brooke helps my mom when she has anxiety attacks. Maybe I can teach you a breathing technique that might help."

"That is super sweet of you; I'll try it. I am just so scared of losing my mates in this battle."

"I go wherever you go, Darah. We will be together and survive." Terrek said confidently.

"You have me here now. I will fry anything that tries to hurt you or your family," Ember said while petting Candy.

"I believe in us. I hate that I let my anxiety consume me sometimes. Ember, will you teach me this breathing thing?"

"Absolutely."

CHAPTER 21

Darah

We were in Stealth Davis, and our first round of fighter pods had just launched. My heart seemed like it had stopped as we started the attack. We were assigned with a fleet to attack Target A on the moon with enslaved women. We came with force, and many Galactic ships were set up around every lead warship. I let go of the breath I was holding when the viewing screen lit up.

"The shit has hit the fan!" I said as the Kanenites engaged.

Once the Kanenites' scans detected us, battleships were launched in droves from the moons that kept their prisoners. It was eerily beautiful, like watching a flock of bird's dance over the waves of the sea.

The ships move stealthily and in perfect formation. The light show that resulted from the laser cannons firing at us was enthralling as Flame evaded the shots. When our ship fired, she hit the first target and the explosion of the battleship had my nerves light up.

In the midst of our fight. Three enemy ships were on us.

Flame was engaging and making maneuvers that would make me ill if it wasn't for the ship's ability to stabilize us. I reached for Terrek's hand as Flame led the command for this fight.

She took out two more ships attacking us. And she took out a ship that was about to hit our allyship. Doing that, though, allowed the third fighter to land a hit on us that had us on a crash course to the moon. Flame, cool as a cucumber, was able to land her shot on that fighter, and it exploded. My girl was the better shot.

"Flame," I cried out as we headed to the surface. We broke through the atmosphere shield, and smoke started to fill the command center.

"Go to the jump pod, leave now!" Flame demanded. She gave Terrek a stern look.

"Take her." Flame said as she looked at us with soft sadness in her eyes.

"No, not without you!" I cried. "

"No, Terrek, grab her too!" I yelled as he dragged me off to a Jump pod.

Ember and Candy were running past us through the smoke. Ember looked me in the eye and said. "Go with Terrek, Darah. I got Candy and Flame."

"No, NO, NOOOOOOO!" I screamed in a panic as Terrek pulled me into a pod, and we jumped away from our burning ship and our mate.

"Why? Terrek, why did you leave her!" I cried.

I felt so betrayed. This was not happening. This can't be happening! We hit hard, my body jerked, my head hit something, and my nose cracked. Blood was pouring out, and that terrible taste of copper filled my mouth. I was numb; shock was taking over.

"Darah, my sweet, I am so sorry. Here, let me help you." He tore off some of his uniform and tried to clean my face.

"Stop, Terrek, I can't believe you left her, left my Candy. What happened to I go wherever you two go?"

"Darah, leaving her was the hardest thing I ever did." He choked up himself.

Terrek's jaw was clenched, and a pulse in his jaw kept a quick rhythm. He wiped a tear from his eye with a roughness. His eyes filled as he stared deeply into my eyes.

"Why?" I cried.

"Flame made me promise to get you to safety. She swore she would be able to focus on saving herself when she doesn't have to worry about saving us, too."

"Terrek, I cannot stand that we left her," I said through tears as he insisted on cleaning my face. He pulls me in for a hug and kisses my head.

"We need to move. We can't stay here. We are on the moon that houses the female slaves." He said as he grabbed our weapons and survival packs.

I left our life pod and saw the spaceships battle above us. I saw a ship falling in a fiery crash further away from us. I hitch my breath in terror.

"I lost my Candy and Flame. How could they have survived a fiery crash?"

Tears fall freely as I notice numbly that I can breathe heavy air. I put on my pack and robotically followed Terrek. My steps kicked up the soft powder-like surface of the grey moon. We landed inside the prison gates. Alarms blared all around us. Debris from the battle above fell all around us.

Terrek pulled me to run with him when I heard our pod explode. it was like running on the beach slower and more difficult as our boots sank with every step. It was dark, but the battle fire lit everything around us. We crouched in the shadow of a doorway that had solid metal doors locked and sealed tight.

I looked at a guard tower, it was firing laser shots into the smoky sky. To my amazement, a giant blue dragon flew into view and lit up that tower with a spray of lava fire. My heart skipped a beat, if Ember survived the crash, Flame and Candy may have managed to survive too.

Hope bloomed in my chest, and my tears turned to cheers as I yelled to Ember, "Burn their asses!" Terrek pulled me back into the shadow.

"Don't alert the enemy to our location." Terrek put me behind him up against the door,

"We need to find Flame and Candy." I tried to push my big male out of my way.

"Darah, focus; were on a mission, we need to follow our training. Flame knows what needs to happen. We need to trust her abilities. I promise I will find them as soon as this fight is over."

I can see Terrek desperately wanted to find them. I knew he was right. I needed to focus. Okay, I needed to blow this door and move on. I pulled my pack off and dug out my magnetic grenade.

"Get ready to move; I am blowing this bitch." Terrek's eyes grew alarmed.

I slapped that device on the door and activated the countdown.

"Damnit, woman, you are mad!" Terrek growled as he pulled me in his arms and ran.

The explosion blasted so much that a percussion wave hit us, and we both flew, hitting the solid metal prison wall hard. Terrek turned his body in time to take the blow.

My breath was knocked out of me. Gasping for air, I held myself on my knees and focused on catching my breath. My lungs burned. Terrek stood up and grabbed my hand. We ran to the broken building. The blast took out more than the door. Two guards ran past us, engulfed in flames.

I thought about shooting a killing laser shot at them, but Terrek kept me moving. We made our way into the prison that kept the females. A blast hit the wall next to us and ricocheted, hitting Terrek in his thigh.

Our armored suits held up for me, but Terrek was hurt. Blood was staining his pant leg. I fired my laser taking out the asshole that injured my Terrek. I scanned the area for more, but the crumbled building had crushed the guards stationed there.

"Can you walk?" I asked Terrek, not looking away from the path before us.

"Yes, keep moving. "Terrek answered with pain laced in his voice.

I could tell he was trying to hide his pain from me. My senses picked up on him. The alarm was blaring, and the smoke and debris had put my awareness on high alert.

I reached the gates that accessed the female holding cells, where a guard desk was located. It looked empty, but a hand came up with a laser and shot at us. Terrek took me down to the ground, and the shot narrowly missed us.

I shot at the desk, my laser powerful enough to shoot right through it, and I heard the male guard grunt as he fell dead against the bars. Terrek retrieved the gate keypad that controlled the locks, pushed the button, and opened the cells.

I walked into the holding area. A tall female stepped out of her cell. She was naked and looked utterly defeated. She was purple like Terrek but had no horns. They looked shorn off with small numbs left.

I felt so sad that we didn't get here to save them sooner. I saw two human-looking females with pointed ears hugging one another as tears brimmed their eyes. These must be Tarinites female.

"I am Darah, and we came to save you and your friends." I held my hands out to show I was not a threat.

Terrek stepped out of the smoke behind me. His limp made it obvious he was hurt.

The female before me noticed Terrek; recognition entered her black eyes.

"Terrek!" She said as she rushed to him.

He gave a tight smile and hugged her briefly before she let go of him and looked at his leg.

"You have been lasered." She said with concern.

"I will heal. It is time we get you all home, Nala." Terrek said.

Tears brimmed his eyes as he saw that her horns were carved off. He pulled back from her and evaluated her with concern. He saw the other females that started to emerge from their cells.

They all looked young, maybe in their twenties. They were all nude, with only a collar on their necks. I gazed into an empty cell and saw bare mats and a toilet. No sheets or clothes.

These females were stripped of all dignity. Bruises darkened spots on their skin, turning purple skin black. Hot anger had my blood boiling. I was pretty sure we hit the sex slave cells.

"These fucking bastards need to burn, every one of them." I spit at the guard I shot and kicked him for good measure.

Ember came into the building, smoke steaming out her nostrils, her naked flesh marked with blue scales. Candy was at her heels with a bloody snout. He was wagging his tale happily. Ember wasn't completely back to her female form. With her blue-scaled body and enlarged claws.

"The evil Kanenites are no match for my dragon flame. What a thrill it is to fight." Ember said with a witty grin.

Her face fell when she sniffed the air. "It smells of fear and sex in here."

"This is the sex slave prison," I said flatly.

Ember turned her head towards the exit and let out a roar that sprayed a blast of fire. Her anger let loose in a spray of lava fire. If any fallen guards had breath left in them, they disintegrated.

"I don't understand this evil," Ember said as she turned around to see all the Laverian females looking at her in shock and awe.

"None of us will ever understand," Terrek said sadly.

"Is Flame safe?" I asked Ember as I held my breath for her answer.

"She sent me to protect you. Some lady named Andromeda

was running from her last I saw. She seemed capable enough. I grabbed Candy, but not before he bit off that female's arm. Not sure how far she will get."

Candy licked his chops as Ember rubbed his big ears. "What an impressive beast you are." She cooed.

"She's alive." I let out a relieved breath. Terrek looked at me with relief as well. Pain creasing his brow together.

"We needed to clear this prison and make sure every bastard guard is dead," I said, putting my head back into the game.

"I will stay here with Candy and guard the entrance," Terrek said.

I could see his injuries taking a toll. Females of Laverian were trying to tend to him even though they suffered themselves.

"Nala, please move the women back to safety. I will be well. There is no need to worry. Please let me guard this spot. Reinforcements are coming. I have friends coming to help save us all." Terrek insisted as the female Nala tried to convince the Laverian females to move back.

My heart ached as I saw the females all injured and traumatized, yet they all wanted to help Terrek.

I pulled out an adrenaline shot, handing it to him in case he needed it later, and I placed a clotting pad on his wound. I kissed him quickly.

"I love you, Terrek. "I said as I turned to clear the building with Ember.

I gave Nala a collar release key and a laser shooter. She quickly started releasing her people.

We cleared the prison easily enough, and my wrist hologram showed us blueprints. We found injured females in a so-called infirmary. They looked to be on death's door, bruised, bloody and unresponsive.

We used the gurneys they laid on to wheel them down to the other females. Their so-called beds were nothing more than body-sized metal trays with wheels. I wish I had a way to offer them coverings and medical aid. For now, that would have to wait.

I went to Terrek and made him sit.

"Time to get off your leg, babe." I tried to get him to lie down. But he refused.

"Ember and these females will help me fight. Besides, we have Candy." I insisted.

We could hear the battle outside. It seemed to be dying down. I could only pray that we would be the victors. Terrek stood up when we heard a ship landing outside.

Terrek, Ember, and I stood ready, facing the opening in the building. Candy stood in-between Ember and I ready to pounce.

"I can hardly believe my eyes. That chetaht is tamed." I heard a Laverian female say to Nala.

"I am just glad it is on our side," Nala said.

Through the smoke, my Flame emerged in her battle form, like a she-devil from hell.

Her wild red eyes scanned until they landed on me, then Terrek.

A collective gasp left the females behind us as Flame marched forward. In her left hand, she held onto a pitiful Andromeda. She tossed her aside like a piece of trash when Candy pounced and ran after Andromeda.

I heard Andromeda let out a weak cry as I ran and jumped into Flame's arms. She held me tight as I kissed her scorching lips. She was so hot I almost felt burned.

"Candy, no, Just guard her," I said as I focused on Flame.

"Don't ever send me away like that again. I lost my mind thinking you died in a fiery crash."

"I love you too." Flame said in a demonic voice.

She was tarnished with grit and dirt, and her suit was ripped on her shoulder. Her markings were golden bright as I watched her completely transform into her normal form. She would frighten me in her battle form if I did not know and love her.

Terrek pulled both of us to him in a tight hug.

"I love you both so much. I do not like having either of you face danger.» Terrek said.

"He is injured," I told Flame, and we broke apart to fuss over Terrek, getting him to sit down again.

Flame's voice and features softened when she focused on Terrek.

The females stepped back, leaving us space cautious of Flame after seeing her battle-form.

"Please don't fear her. She is with us." I pleaded with the scared females.

"Don't get defensive, Darah. I would worry if they did not fear me in my battle form." Flame soothed me with her soft voice.

"I am not sure I will ever get used to your battle form," I said with a wink as we made Terrek take a sip of energy water.

"We have defeated the Kanenites on this moon. I am waiting for transport ships to be escorted in to retrieve the formerly enslaved people. I need to let them know we need robes as many as possible.

I'll Have them report back to me. Flame demanded as more of our warriors entered the prison. It wasn't long before the medical teams arrived and issued robes and water. We stayed until the last female was escorted and left with them to the transport ships waiting above the moon's atmosphere."

I felt relief wash over me as I had my Flame and Terrek beside me. I sent up a prayer of thanks to the Goddess Harmony. *Thank you for keeping us alive.*

Ember was petting Candy, a very tender moment in contrast to the blood that coated Candie's muzzle. The two seemed to be finding comfort in the aftermath of the battle.

I feel gratitude for being alive with my family safe and being able to help rescue these enslaved females. Witnessing the horror of what they endured will haunt me for the rest of my life. I plan on helping them however I can from here on out.

"I am getting reports that the other attacks are going in our favor. We hit them by surprise." Flame said.

"Thank you, Flame, for saving my people and all those who were slaves. Terrek said.

"Medic!" Flame cried out as Terrek passed out and fell into her arms.

CHAPTER 22

Flame

I cannot believe I let that fucking laser hit us. Shit! We were going down.

I hit the evacuation button. My crew would eject in the pods. I needed to kill that Kanenites asshole to give us more time. I lined the enemy ship up and fired. Yes! I'd shoot it twice if I could vaporize that ass again, just for the inconvenience of having to crash my girl's ship. I looked at Terrek. I gave him the nod, signaling that he would escape with Darah.

"Go to the jump pod. Leave now!" I yelled at Terrek. I could see the pain in his eyes.

We discussed this, and he promised me. For a second, I thought he would grab me, too. He better not. I need to save whoever cannot make it to the eject pods.

"Take her," I said.

I was glancing at Darah as she broke my heart. She was crying to get me. I love those two. ‹*Goddess Dammit! You better not let me die. I am not ready to leave them yet. We just barely started.*› I prayed.

Okay, it was time to focus. My heart pounded, and I locked onto the pod carrying my mates. My wrist communicator will now be able to locate them. I sent an alert to the fighters that were assigned to flank me. They knew that protecting my mate's pod was a priority.

Damn this thing. It must be the Kanenites' engineering because this was a piece of shit compared to the Galactic ships. The upgrades I installed were the only reason I could keep flying, but barely.

Most of my crew had ejected. Fuck, here we go. "You gotta be fucking kidding me!"

I pull hard to maneuver the ship with an extended and engaged manual joystick. Meaning we were screwed. Ember ran through the smoke with Candy in tow. Great, just great! Another stubborn female who doesn›t obey orders. I would reem her ass if I weren›t out of Time.

"Brace yourself for impact!"

Was all I could get out when Ember morphed with her wings exploding from her back. She grabbed the beast, Candy, and me. She wrapped us up in a cocoon of her tuff wings.

Ember's arms suddenly wrapped around me, and I was cocooned tightly with Candy wrapped up in leathery wings. I felt the scales rubbing my cheek raw and the sudden thunder and jolt of the crash. The Ship bounced and skid to a stop.

Ember had us protected in her wings. She rolled to unfurl her wings and let Candy and me free of her embrace.

I stood in the smoke and transformed into my battle form. Ember grabbed Candy and used her wings to cover him as she ran through the fire. I ran after her, the fire licking my body but not scorching me. As soon as I made it outside the ship, Kanenites, and Galactic fighters were engaged in a laser blast fight above us. An enemy ground transport was heading our way, firing at us.

Ember transformed into a vast blue dragon. Incredible! I thought her wings were excellent inside the ship, but this beast was a new level of badass. I dodged a laser from a craft above.

My Galactic Warriors made a hit on that asshole. The ship exploded, and shrapnel flew at me.

Fuck!» I yelled as I hit the sandy surface of this moon, going prone and covering my neck.

My new dragon friend flapped her wings so hard I was dragged a few feet on the surface while that ship's debris was blown away. I owe her. I can't handle another spinal injury. Ember was blowing her fire at the Kanenites' ships. Where can I recruit a fleet of these dragons? I stood up and felt a brutal hit to the back of my ribs.

I have had it with this bitch! Andromeda was attacking me. I turned and raked my finger claws across her face. The deep scorch of my fingers wounded her face. My nails marked her face forever with my strike. The look on Andromeda's face was comical. She wasn't expecting my battle form. Fear reached her malicious features as she evaluated me.

Now I understand how Candy feels, wanting to kill this chick.

"That's right, run, make this fun, you evil shit," I growled in my monstrous battle-form voice.

In the event of a crash, the core power system shuts down, allowing the stasis containment to be awoken and set free. It›s too bad in this case. Now Andromeda was on the run.

The dragon burned the ground transport and picked it up, tossing it into three flying fighters like blazing cannons. The three ships crashed, and she set them ablaze.

Candy ran past me as he chased after Andromeda. He pounced and latched onto her arm. Part of me was disappointed I didn't get to her first. I ran up to them.

"Please don't let him kill me!"

"Good boy, Candy, it's not time to kill her yet." I reached for Andromeda and yanked her to her feet. Candy did not let go of his hold on her arm. When he pulled away, her arm came with him. He hissed and roared at her, pointing his tail. The threat was so intense I got a fisher of fear. Shaking it off, I held Andromeda in a tight grip. I slapped a clotting pad on her shoulder's severed arm wound.

Defeated and resigned to being my captive, Andromeda went limp as I dragged her behind me.

A couple of Kanenites manage to escape their burning crashed ship. Candy ran after them next. He pounced on one and stung the other with his tail. I felt like he was taking out his aggression on the enemy. Giving my captive a view of how vicious he could be.

Terrek tried to warn me of the chetaht predator, but nothing could prepare me for this sight. The gore from his powerful bites and claws I get, but the guy that was melting from the inside out after that stinger tail struck. Now, he looks like he was dipped in acid. Gross! That was indeed a dangerous stinger. I was so glad that Candy liked me.

Andromeda may be an asset since her father was so high-ranking in this universe. I pulled her to the prison wall and checked the clotting pad. She screamed from the pain.

The wall surrounding the prison was a cold reminder that my mates were inside. I noticed the atmospheric towers as a ship had almost crashed into them. I wonder how long we could breathe if the tower were destroyed.

With a new urgency, I placed a demolishing grenade on the wall. Running away, dragging this woman with me. The wall exploded. The sky was filling up with more and more Galactic ships, we are taking the lead over this battle.

As I breached the wall, I was ambushed in hand-to-hand combat. Dropping Andromeda, I heard her weakly cry out to be saved by her kind. Ember and Candy joined me in our ground fight.

"Take Candy and Find my mates, I ordered. I will be there shortly. They may need backup more than I do."

Ember looked around briefly, accessing my opponents. She shrugged and took Candy to help my mates. Knowing that dragon and Candy would protect my loves, something inside my chest calmed. I faced the enemy before me and let my finger spray my fires out. Molten liquid set blaze to the beings that thought they had a chance when they attacked me.

A mass of Kanenites rushed me, and I lost my captive in the swarm of beings that engaged me. I set off another grenade, and bodies blew apart all around me. A galactic fighter ship gave me cover. I broke free of the ambush and recovered Andromeda, who had been abandoned and left lying on the grey powdery surface of the moon. I ran for the prison and my mates.

I saw several Kanenites ships launching off the moon and taking heavy fire. Most crashed in a fiery blaze, and one or two slipped by. I entered the building and went through a maze of smoke and rubble.

Finally, I saw my mates surrounded by the nude females held here. The sight made me want to return to the fight and execute more savagery to the evil kind that would treat beings this way.

One way or another, I will prevail in this war. Candy pounced once again, this time to greet me with slobbery kisses. I was glad he is worthy and on my side. I gave him a quick pat on his head as I saw my Darah, her nose swollen and her uniform bloody and frayed. She ran into my arms.

Don›t ever send me away like that again. I lost my mind thinking you died in a fiery crash.» She said to me in tears.

How did I get this lucky to have her and her pure love for me? I looked over at Terrek while I hugged her. The love that shined in his eyes melted me.

"I love you too," I said to Darah, meaning it, and I felt bad I hurt her by sending her away. Their safety was always my priority, so I could not promise I wouldn't do it again if needed.

This battle was wrapping up. I sent orders to salvage Darah's things from the ship I crashed. I know that the guitar and her sack from Earth are essential to her. I felt bad I crashed her ship. I knew she claimed it and was proud to have it as hers. It was her new home, and I wanted her to have it her way. Her happiness was important to me.

We made our way to the triage rescue ship. Those females needed a lot of assistance to heal from this imprisonment. My reports showed favorable odds for us in this war. I really can't stand a tyrant. I was feeling so grateful that we survived and had a successful mission. I just mentioned something to my mates about the reports I was getting.

"Thank you, Flame, for saving my people and all those who were slaves," Terrek said.

He passed out and fell into my arms, realizing he was injured badly. My fear for him replaced any rational thought.

"Medic!" I cried.

"Terrek, baby, why didn't you tell us you were hurt this badly." I cried as I lowered him to the floor.

"Terrek, oh my god, no!" Darah cried as she sank next to his other side.

I pulled off his boots and lost my breath, revealing a bloody wound. When a pool of blood poured out like a wave all over me and the floor. Franticly, I pulled another clotting pad and placed it on his thigh. The Clotting pad failed him. He lost too much blood, and the wound was bigger than the pad.

"Terrek, don't leave me, fight Terrek, fight!" I cried.

The medics pulled Darah and me away from Terrek. I growled as I transformed and barely stopped myself from striking out to get to Terrek. Ember stepped in and contained me. She is probably the only thing strong enough to do so now. Darah's sobs only amplified my pain.

"Calm! Flame." Ember ordered in my ear.

All rational thought was gone. Fear and anger had made me wild. I had never lost it like this before. Part of me could hear Darah crying. Most of me was scared for Terrek.

Darah reached for me. Her touch gave me a piece of sanity back, just enough to snap out of it.

CHAPTER 23

Darah

"This can't be happening!" I cried as they took Terrek away and Flame transformed into her she-devil battle-form. Ember held Flame against her, grabbing Flame from behind. Flame was genuinely terrifying at that moment.

I sank to the floor in my despair. Candy was on me, trying to soothe me. I was seized with fear. I could not lose any more family. I wanted to be there for Flame, too.

'Please, Harmony, save him!' I Prayed so hard in my haze of shock and fear.

I hugged Candy and sank my face into his furry shoulder. I felt his scratchy tongue licking me. I took a deep breath of air that burned my lungs, and then another and another.

I was relieved we were on the refugee ship. I knew this ship had infirmaries and medical units on every level. Finally starting to get my bearings, I looked up and saw Ember struggling to keep Flame from escaping her hold.

I needed to be here for her, strong for all of us. I stood up and rushed to Flame. I cupped her face to help her calm down. He needs us." I softly pleaded with her.

I just held her in my hands and softly repeated my plea. I felt the tension in Flame melt away as she relaxed. Ember released her, and Flame hugged me tightly as she sobbed in my arms. Moments passed, and I slowly pulled back to look into her sad red eyes. I caught the tear that fell on her cheek.

He will fight to stay with us,» I promised because I couldn't face anything less.

Flame softened, and her form morphed into her usual self.

"Yes, you're right. We need to go check on him." Flame said sadly.

Holding my hand as we went to see how Terrek was doing. Ember and Candy trailed just steps behind us. Everyone around us had fallen eerily silent as they watched us walk.

I can feel them worry for us. All this energy was too overwhelming. I squeezed Flame's hand as we walked. She gave me a silent look, her red eyes swollen from crying.

"We look a mess, you and me. I am just glad we are together. Terrek must be okay. He will survive this. Our healers are the best of the best." Flame reassured me.

We walked past a window where I got a glimpse of my reflection. My nose was swollen, and I was sure I had broken it. Blood and grime still smeared on my cheeks.

"I did a number on myself," I mentioned as we came to a small crowd of medical personnel who blocked the door to the following medical room.

"A little blood and dirt are expected in a battle. I think you are brave and beautiful, my Earthling." Flame let go of me and wiped at my dirty cheek. She gave me a quick kiss before we went to be with Terrek.

"How is he?" Flame demanded in her commander's voice, back to business.

A male with half of his face humanoid and the other was mechanical. He looked robotic, standing over seven feet tall. He broke through the people standing at the infirmary door.

"Make way. I want the mates to enter." I heard his deep, robotic voice boom.

I pushed my intrigue to the side. My whole focus was on Terrek. This man was the healer holding my mate's life in his hands. Flame gave the man a nod as we came to Terrek's bedside.

I choked up, holding back my tears as I looked at him. Such a vast male was lying there, fading right in front of us.

"I am a healer, C-MD, in the 1st class, Major Zako, a doctor. I have stopped his bleeding and given him fluids. He is under a constant scan. His readings show that he has fractured ribs.

A laser wound has nicked the arteries located in his upper thigh. I have clamped his artery for now. We must act fast to give him blood. We have females from Laverian claiming to be his cousins who wanted to donate their blood to save him.»

Two robed Laverian females entered the room, interrupting Doctor Zako.

Excuse me, no time to explain.» The doctor swiftly turned his attention to the females, scanning them with a handheld device.

"Miss, please lay on this bed so my nurse can start the blood withdrawal." He picked one female to lie down.

My heart was worried and grateful for all these people trying to save my big purple mate. The females teared up, looking at Terrek.

He is my cousin. I am willing to do whatever it takes to save him. I am unsure if my blood is clean after . . . my imprisonment. Please save him, doctor."

The female said with tears. The emotions in the room were swamping me. Taking a deep breath, I tried to control my feelings. I was grateful for this team working to save Terrek.

"We are forever in your debt for saving our mate." Flame said to Terrek's cousin.

"Of course, he is family. You are family now, too. No need to repay me." The female said.

I looked at the bruises on her exposed body, and my heart hurt for her and what she must have endured. Here, she was offering her blood to save Terrek when she hadn't even been treated for her injuries yet. These people were truly phenomenal. The cyborg doctor robotically listed off the reading of his scan to the female.

"Your blood is low on vitamins. You've been malnourished. You have internal damage. Tearing, and you have been severely beaten in your stomach. The implant to sterilize you was damaged by the beating of your stomach. You carry a positive pregnancy. There is damage to your throat due to strangulation attempts. Your retina in your left eye is damaged."

The female's purple skin darkened, and her eyes teared up with fear.

"Excuse me, Doctor. Stop!" I said, interrupting his vocal evaluation. I walked to the lady and asked,

"Can I hold your hand?" She reached for my hand in answer.

"I am Darah. This is my mate Flame. What is your name?"

"Tinah." The female choked out. She looked at us with panic in her teary eyes.

"Tinah, we are so grateful to you for helping us save Terrek. You are our family now. I am so sad we had to meet like this. Just know we are here for you, and you are safe. Don't be scared. You will be okay. We will get you the support you need."

The cyborg, the doctor, was oblivious to the room's emotions as he focused on his patient.

"Female Tinah of Laverian, you require medical assistance. I will not take your blood. Nurse Jax is a female who specializes in fertility counseling. She will take you to another physician to attend to your injuries and offer different medical options.

Termination of your pregnancy with counseling is offered to help you cope. You can Donate your fetus to be held in cryo freeze for a later pregnancy or adopt the cryo fetus out.

You can carry your pregnancy, keep or offer your child up for adoption. You will be healed, and treatment will be your choice." His robotic voice was explaining to Tinah.

"I am your nurse. My name is Jax. I am going to wheel your bed to your room. I will give you updates on your cousin Terrek." Tinah looked relieved to have Jax take her.

"We will come to see you as soon as we know Terrek is stable," I said as she was wheeled out of the room.

My heart broke for her and her situation. The second female was already lying on her bed, being scanned. I looked at her as she looked scared seeing Tinah leave the room. I wished that this Cyborg Doctor had better bedside manners.

"What is your name?" I asked as her bed was moved closer to Terrek's bed.

"I am Tam." She said as the Dr. was in his scanning analysis mode. "I can hold your hand if you are comfortable?" I offered.

"You have the infertile implant like your sister. However, yours is in working order. You are negative without pregnancy. You are malnourished, have internal tearing, and have bruises. You are stable enough to donate blood."

"After we collect the blood, we will send you to another physician to guide you through the treatment. You have the option for your implant to be removed and your injuries worked on in the way you choose. You will be assigned your nurse for counseling and aftercare needs. Thank you for your assistance."

This cyborg guy had a terrible way of approaching his patients, but I was so worried about Terrek that I knew I had to endure it. As long as everyone gets the best care. Blood was drawn, and Tam was moved out of the room.

"Thank you, Tam. We will check on you and your sister soon." Flame said, and I gave Tam my grateful smile.

"Can we reprogram this cyborg doctor so he is not so traumatizing to people who have been through so much already? "I asked Flame in a whisper.

"I have never met one so blunt and emotionless before. I will look into it once things settle." Flame assured me.

The doctor started to give Terrek the blood, and as soon as the blood hit his veins, he started convulsing.

"Oh my God, what is happening?" I cried as Flame pulled me close for a tight hug as we watched the doctor work on Terrek.

"His body is rejecting the blood. My analysis shows he has been altered."

"What do you mean altered?" Flame demanded.

The doctor turned to face us and pointed his handheld scan at us. After a moment, he spoke.

"Commander Flame, you have marked your mates, and with your venom, you have altered their DNA so they can have reproductive compatibility with you.

He needs fire blood, but you have nanos that complicate donations. Gias fire blood won't work, and yours is too hot for his system."

I am beginning to dislike this doctor. He was blunt, robotic, and not helpful with all this bad news.

Flame melted into me, crying on my neck.

"I have doomed him with my altered blood." She sobbed softly.

"No, Flame, you mated to us. He would never change that. There has to be a way."

I held her as I heard Ember push her way into the room.

"Move. I am needed." Ember made her way to us.

"I have enhanced hearing. I have been pacing in the halls with Candy. I can smell things better than you can. I have fire blood. I smelled your blood the moment I met you. See if my blood will work. Take what I offer freely."

Ember held her bare arm out to the cyborg. Doctor Zako scanned her.

Intriguing. I have never seen your blood type before.»

He proceeded to take her blood and transfuse it to Terrek.

The blood hit his veins, and he took her blood without reaction. Once, he was given as much blood as Ember could spare.

His body started to heal from the inside out. The wound pushed the clamp out of his thigh, and his body became whole. Flame and I pulled Ember in for a tight group hug, "You did it. You saved him." I said.

"I owe you, my dragon friend. Words cannot say what this means to me." Flame said.

"It was a simple thing to offer my blood. Please, I am just glad it worked." Ember hugged us back and exited the room to wait with Candy.

I went to one side of Terrek's bed while Flame went to the other. We each held his hand and leaned down to kiss him.

"Her blood healed him . . . It is like magic. I have never seen such a thing." The doctor said in his robotic voice.

He conveyed genuine shock, the first emotion I could detect from him.

"Yes, our gal Ember is something made of magic," I said, not taking my eyes off Terrek.

I heard Ember laughing in the hall. "These beings are silly, right Candy?"

Terrek opened his sleepy eyes. He looked at me, then Flame, "What happened?"

He said, confused.

"It doesn't matter. All I care about is that you are well and alive." I said, happy to see his black eyes.

"Darah of Earth, I need to attend to your nose." Doctor Zako interrupted my perfect moment.

"I am fine, don't worry about me," I said.

Terrek sat up and demanded, "Doctor, heal my mate."

Flame said, "Your turn, babe."

"Fine!" I gave in and turned to face a new device placed over my face.

My nose was set straight, and we were finally left in the medical room to be alone.

CHAPTER 24

Darah

Terrek escorted Flame and me to check on his cousins Tinah and Tam. This medical ship was massive, a small city floating in space. We entered the room that the sisters shared. Tinah and Tam got up and gave Terrek a big hug.

"Thank you for trying to help save me." He said affectionately.

We settled in our seats.

"How are you two recovering? Is everyone treating you well?" I asked.

"Yes, I am better after the initial shock of finding out I was pregnant. I chose to cryo freeze the fetus for now. I am talking with my very supportive counselor."

"I am not sure if I will allow adoption or terminate yet, but I am comfortable with it staying in cryo for now. It will give me time to come to terms. I know I just wanted it out of me."

"I can't imagine how hard this all is. I am glad you are happy with your care. You look so much better already." I said.

"Yes, we have been given fluids to replenish our needs and speed up the healing. The laser repair machine handled all the tearing, so I am tender but much better now. So happy to be going home." Tam said.

"Do you know of my parents?" Terrek asked.

Tinah gave Terrek a sad look before she softly spoke.

"Terrek, your father was killed fighting to protect us. He fell with the warriors who fought with him. You are now chief, my cousin Terrek."

"And my mother?" Terrek said with a choked-up voice. His black eyes filled with sadness.

"We females were separated. They took her to the servant assimilation camp," Tam said.

"She was considered too old for sex service. I hope she was spared the troubles we endured." Tinah spoke softly.

"I need her name; I will check to see if we have rescued her." Flame insisted.

"Oh, honey, I am sorry this happened to your father." I put my hand on Terrek's thigh to offer comfort while he buried his face in his hands in sorrow.

"Thank you for telling us. We need to take Terrek to our room so he can process the news." Flame said as she logged Terrek's mother's name into her wrist communicator.

"Tora is a beautiful name, Terrek. We will find your mom," I whispered as he stoically stood up, and we went to our room.

"My purple love, I will find your mother." Flame vowed to prioritize another mission.

"I will meet you two back in our room. I need to check on a few things." Flame kissed me, then gave Terrek a sweet, long, lingering kiss.

"I am so sorry for your loss, my love; I wish I could have met your father." Flame softly said as she reluctantly pulled away.

The slow walk to our assigned room was blurry as I silently supported Terrek. He was sad and recovering. There were two smaller beds in this room. This unit felt foreign, and

I felt homesick for my lost ship. I put on a brave face and guided Terrek to our bed.

Terrek was heartbroken by the news of his father and worried about his mother. He softly cried in my arms and told me about the last moments he remembered with his father. I just wanted to comfort him and support him through the pain.

I was grateful he was alive, and that was everything then. Pulling back the thin bedding, we settled on one of the beds. I wrapped my body around him and gently scratched his body, landing kisses on his arm as we lay there until we fell asleep.

I woke up to Terrek's gentle kiss.

"I love my sweet Darah, but I must get up to relieve myself," he said with puffy eyes.

I moved off the bed so he could get up to use the bathroom. Rubbing my eyes and yawning, I stretched, noticing Flame was not here yet.

"What time is it?" I asked.

"I am not sure; I think Flame is still working. She does too much, especially after that battle. We should go find her." Terrek said as he went to get dressed.

"Agreed, she needs to be with us. We all need to be together." I said as we left the room.

I felt guilty for sleeping all snuggled up next to Terrek as Ember continued to work. I assumed she would be joining us shortly after we laid down. I should have known better.

A guard stood outside in the hall by our door.

"Empress Darah of Laverian, Commander Flame of Gia, has assigned me to keep you safe. I am officer Stella of Gia." The tall brunette female said.

"Officer Stella, can you please take us to Commander Flame?"

We followed behind Stella as she led the way through the massive ship to an area where viewing screens and holographs were displayed on every wall and table. Flame sat at a table with several other high-ranking beings. One male was another cyborg. He was plugged into the port on the table.

I was dizzy with all the star maps and displays showing different ships, moons, and planets.

Another female with stern features used her fingers to zoom in on the display in front of herself and Flame.

"These evil beings are vile; look, there are more prisons in this system over here." The stern-looking woman showed Flame.

"I see the horror of evil all over this universe. However, we must focus on our mission and return our rescued. We must fortify our borders and reinforce protection barriers around our galactic universe. We cannot invade deeper into the Kanenites universe, at least not anytime soon." Flame said to the irritated female.

"I am sorry to interrupt, but my mate has not yet rested after her battle. I insist it's time for Flame to have her sleep cycle." Terrek announced firmly.

Flame turned towards Terrek and me; her face softened, and her tired eyes smiled when she saw us.

Flame stood to pull us into a big hug. "I am so happy to see you up and healthy," she said to Terrek, kissing him deeply.

"We missed you in our bed," I whispered as I kissed her next.

"I know I got held up, but I promise to return to our room shortly. Please head back. I will be right there without delay this time." Flame winked.

"MMM, female, you better hurry," Terrek growled and smacked Flame's sexy ass as she walked away.

"I hate to see her leave, but I sure love that view," I said, teasing Terrek, hoping it would help ease his broken heart.

He leaned down to kiss me in a lingering kiss.

"I am truly blessed to have you two. Thank you for being so kind to my cousins. Thank you for all this, Darah. My whole world was doomed to a nightmare. You popped into my world and became mine. Then you found us, Flame, and the Galactic Empire working to free my people.

We both have lost a lot, but we have also gained the

impossible. I know I can rebuild, and I have hope for all of us. You did this." Terrek said as he waved his hand to encompass the scurry of people going this way and that. Everyone was working to help.

"I don't feel like I did all this, Terrek. We did it together and will continue to work together no matter what life throws our way. I am so glad we won that battle and rescued so many. We need to go home and rebuild."

We entered our small, assigned quarters. Candy rested in the corner. Terrek moved the beds together so all of us would fit. This left little walk room, but we didn't care. I sat on the bed next to Terrek when we heard a knock on the door.

Ember stepped in when I opened the door.

"Hi, Darah. I am happy I am here to help but worried about my family. I need to speak with Harmony."

"I am so sorry you have been taken away from your world, Ember, But I am so grateful for you being here. You saved Flame and Candy, and then you saved Terrek."

My whole world is alive because of you. I only see Harmony in my dreams. Sometimes, I see my family with her too. I don't know how to take you to Harmony in my dreams. However, I can promise to ask her how to return you to your home the next time I dream of her."

"I want to speak with Harmony. Can I ask you to let me hold your hand while you sleep so I can try to see Harmony?" Ember asked.

"If you want a sleepover so you can hold my hand, hell, that's the least I can do. Done, I will come to stay with you tonight."

"Thank you, Darah. It's good to see you, Terrek, and you, my favorite fur buddy," Candy rubbed against Ember's body.

"Can I take him to play for a bit, he looks like he can barely fit in this room?"

"Yes, of course. I will see you tonight." I said as Ember left with Candy at her heels.

"That is one incredible female," Terrek said.

"You are one incredible male," I said as I entered his arms. He pulled me in for a passionate kiss.

His horns were the best. I grabbed on and wrapped myself around him. He laid me on the bed, and we just got lost in each other's lips.

Flame entered our room. Terrek broke our kiss and reached over me, beckoning Flame to join us. Her red eyes turned hungry, and she took his hand. She crawled next to us, sandwiching me between them.

"I think this might be my favorite spot," I said as I felt Flame remove her shirt and press her subtle soft breast against my back.

"You two are way too dressed." Flame said as she kissed the back of my neck. I loved it when she did that.

"Too much clothing," Terrek growled low and sexy.

I rolled into her silky arms. "Mmm, I love the way you kiss me." I let my hands roam over her sexy body.

Terrek made quick work of taking off his clothes. He drew our attention when he moaned, looking at Flame and me kissing. He grabbed his huge cock and worked it as he watched us.

"Don't stop. I am thoroughly enjoying the view," Terrek said in his sexy voice.

"Don't worry, stud. We got you." I said as I bent my head to suck on Flame's pebbled nipple.

Flame moaned and reached for Terrek, taking him in her mouth and sucking him up and down his shaft.

"Fuck, those hot lips of yours, Flame, you're killing me." He grabbed her bound hair and helped her with the rhythm he wanted. I took a moment to undress.

"Flame, you must stop, or I will easily lose it." Terek pulled her off his cock with her mouth popping away from him. She looked up at him in a haze of lust.

I leaned over to kiss Flame. She tasted like Terrek's flavor on her tongue. I let her kiss leave my lips so she could kiss Terrek as he crawled into our bed.

He pulled Flame into him as he spooned her from behind. She reached for me and pulled my head to her breast as she turned her head back to kiss Terrek.

I played with her sexy tits in my mouth. I felt her reach for me. I looked into her red eyes and Terrek's black eyes. They were mine, and that moment was so beautiful to me. I leaned in to kiss Flame. I felt the moment Terrek entered her.

"Mmmh." He moaned as he started moving. Flame exhaled a sexy breath, breaking our kiss. I kissed down her body, her legs spreading as he took her from behind. The sight was sexy as hell. I leaned down to lick her clit as he penetrated her.

"Oh Fuck, that feels so good," Flame moaned as her body bounced.

I love the way she tastes and her reaction to us touching her.

"I am cumming." Flame moaned as she vibrated with her orgasm.

"Me too!" Terrek growled out a husky moan as he pulsed his seed into her at the same time.

Terrek slowly left Flame as she maneuvered me to lay back. She took her freshly swollen clit and puts her pussy up to mine. Clamping her long, sexy legs with mine.

This is the first time I have ever tried the scissor position. My body was drenched with need. Terrek leaned down to kiss me, and he played with our breasts.

"Fuck!" I heard him moan as Flame and I started to grind into each other.

Terrek was gripping his still-hard cock. I wanted to suck it, but Flame had me so into her. I was wrapped up in the feeling of bliss. He would have to enjoy the view for now.

"OH God, yes!" I cried out with a moan as I went over the edge, my wet pussy grinding into Flames. This was out of this world for me.

"Yes!" "Mmmm," I heard Flame moan as she came next. I love the flush on her face.

Just when I thought we would break apart to get our hands on Terrek. I felt Flames Pussy muscles grip mine like a suction.

"Oh Damn, that's new." I managed as my sensitive clit was worked enough to send me over the edge again.

"Oh, Darah!" Flame moaned. We were attached, pussy to pussy, scissoring each other as we ground together, building another orgasm. I was in a haze of lust and orgasms.

I felt her bite on my leg, the one she was hugging as we moved together, adding to my bliss. We came hard and stayed attached to one another as our pussies had latched together in some fire-blood way. After a few breathtaking moments, we detached from one another, and Flame crawled up my body and pulled me into her arms, panting in the aftermath.

"Darah, baby, I may have made you pregnant." Flame said breathlessly.

I gently kissed her neck, rubbing my hands all over her body, loving the aftermath of our sex.

"Wait, what did you just say?" I pulled back to look into Flame's eyes, confused.

I did not expect that reaction, but for my species, females can impregnate other females if they attach like that. Our egg travels to the other female's egg, making only girl babies.

I am sorry. I just thought we would have no worries since you are an Earthling. I figure Terrek would father our children in the future."

Our mood shifted to a mixture of happiness and a bit of shock. Terrek sank next to us.

"That was the most stunning orgasm. Would you be thrilled if a baby was just made?" Flame asked excitedly.

"A baby?" Okay, my mind was blown. Flame could impregnate me. How did I feel about that? I looked at Flame and her concerned red eyes. And Terrek and his radiant, loving eyes.

"I love you both so much! If we make babies together, I will be so happy." I said and leaned in to kiss Flame, who looked relieved at my reaction.

"I love you, Darah," Flame said, kissing me softly.

"I love you both so much," Terrek said as he laid back down and pulled me beside him. Terrek just held us, and we all took turns kissing.

"Terrek, you didn't get to cum with me that time.?" I said as we all lay together, relaxing.

"Oh, I enjoyed both of you. I will have my turn again another time. Tonight is perfect just the way it is."

"Could he be more perfect?" I asked Flame.

"You both are perfect!" Flame said.

"I am so happy right now. I hate to leave, but I promised Ember I would try to take her into my dream to talk with the Goddess. Ember thinks it would work if she held my hand while we slept." I was going to assume whatever magic she has will make this happen.

I kissed each of them and stood to get dressed.

"Maybe you two can make a baby, too," I said as Flame kissed me, starting that fire again. I moved back with a grittiness and got dressed. I kissed Terrek.

"Make her so tired that she has to sleep for several hours," I said with a wink.

Flame snuggled up to Terrek. The sight of them intertwined together made my heart flutter with love.

"I think I might have to have my way with him." Flame said.

"Threaten me with a good time. I won't complain," Terrek responded.

"I love you both. Have fun!" I laughed as the door closed behind me.

I left my lovers to play for the rest of the night. I was looking forward to seeing my Candy and hanging out with Ember.

CHAPTER 25

Terrek

Flame's body gave Darah the fertility seal. I learned this by using an educator to learn more about Gia's fire blood species. Flame had an implant with Nano lava in her blood that complicates things now that she has been altered.

I was not sure of my fertility compatibility with Flame or Darah. I could only pray that our bond would find a way if the Gods saw fit; we would be compatible to make babies. Seeing that Flame had a successful fertility seal gave me hope.

I needed to ensure the safety of my world, my people, and my family. So we could live a happy, safe life without fear of invasion again. The feeling of my mates lying in bed with me and feeling their love for me and each other was beyond anything I could ever ask for.

We kissed Darah goodbye before she left for her sleepover with our new friend Ember.

"Come here, my fire-blood," I said as I pulled my sexy Flame over me.

"MMM, now that I have you just where I want you." Flame straddled me, her hot pussy teasing my hard cock.

Her red eyes were sultry and hungry, God damn! I was a lucky male.

"Terrek, If I do this, I may be ripe for fertility after sealing with Darah."

"I am thrilled about having children with you two. If you are not ready, we can just lay here together." I asked her.

"I am ready. I just don't want you to be surprised." Flame grabbed my cock and slid herself down.

"You feel hot and tight. I am already worked up." I moaned as I felt her grip me.

She leaned down and kissed me, giving me a slow grind. We came together, and she gripped me with her fertility seal this time too.

"Oh, Fuck!" This was mind-blowing Flame struck her fangs in my neck, giving me a dose of her venom.

"Mmmmm." I moaned, "Flame." I came harder than ever, my shaft pulsing every drop of seed in me. We both came slowly back to our senses.

Flame peppered kisses back up from my neck to my lips. I kissed her deeply, praying my seed took. Showing her without words how much she meant to me.

"I love you, Flame."

"I love you, my big purple beast." She kissed me again, then rolled off me.

I got up to clean myself and to clean her.

"Not this time Terrek. I want your seed to take." She stopped me.

"Come here. Let me hold you." Flame beckoned me to lie back down.

I pulled her into my arms as we lay there in the aftermath of lovemaking.

"Terrek, I found your mother, Taro." She said

"Thank you, Flame. Is she well?"

Of course, she found my mother. She was fantastic. I knew

she would always fight for us, and she would prioritize our family. What a formidable team we make.

"She is alive." Flame kissed my chest.

"We will be arriving in Laverian tomorrow. I have arranged for your family and us to be the first to land tomorrow. Everything else will follow after you have had a moment to reconnect with your family first."

"Our family, Flame. You and Darah are my family. I am happy to introduce my mates to them. They will love you and Darah so much for loving me. Also, for saving us all." I insisted

"I feel like you and Darah have given me a life I never expected. I was married to my job and dedicated to being a warrior. With my implant, I never expected love and family. I was only ever good at war tactics. Now, I want to retire from my position.

I want to stay on Laverian and raise babies with you and Darah, using my skills to protect Laverian. I have submitted my request to command Laverian defenses so I can live there with my mates." Flame stated.

"I just assumed you would be with us. I am sorry I did not discuss this with you sooner. I am so happy you are finding a way to be with us at Laverian. Are you going to miss your home?" I grew tense inside thinking about Flame living on Gia and not with us on Laverian. The thought had never crossed my mind before.

"My home is where you and Darah are. I will not miss Gias. it is easy to visit when I need to. My happiness is with you two and our future." She kissed my bare chest some more.

"I love you, Flame. I am the luckiest male."

"Flame, I know your mom is Empress Zion but you haven't spoken of your father. Will you tell me of him?"

"I have no father, Terrek; my mom was sealed with my other mother, Spark. I don't have a memory of my birthing mother because she was killed in battle when I was a toddler."

"I am so sorry to hear that she passed away, I would have wanted to meet both your parents."

"Thank you Terrek, I know my mom Zion will love her new role as grandma once our babies come. life is about to be everything we dreamed of."

"Get some sleep, my fire, you need to be well rested." I kissed her and pulled her in close to me.

Tomorrow I would be home with my mates and family, and I could start rebuilding. *'Thank you, Goddess Harmony.'* I sent a silent prayer before falling asleep with Flame in my arms.

CHAPTER 26

Darah

I hoped Terrek and Flame enjoyed their time together that night. I was ready to sleep and expected to see my family and get answers for Ember. The guard, Stella, escorted me to Ember's door. I knocked and she answered with a sleepy smile.

I almost fell asleep waiting. I thought you would miss tonight.» Ember seemed surprised to see me.

"I had to spend quality time with my Loves. We all needed it." I said.

I looked at Candy, who was sleeping on a blanket in the corner.

"Wow, you must have played with him hard today. He didn't even wake up to greet me."

"Yes, I made him a fetch toy. We had a blast. I think he wore me out, and that is saying something." Ember sighed.

"You have my backpack and guitar!" I noticed my stuff placed neatly on a table.

"Yes, a soldier was taking it to your room to give it to Flame. She was directly ordered on a special mission to retrieve it. I stopped her and told her I would see to it that you got it first thing in the morning.

She was adamant that she would do her duty as ordered. She relented when I shadowed scales and steam rolled out my nose. She will be filing a grievance on me for my actions, by the way.» Ember snickered.

"Flame is always taking steps to provide what we need. Gods, I love her. Thank you, Ember, for taking my things. We needed privacy earlier. I will make sure Flame drops that grievance case against you. You are a good friend."

"I am happy to help. I am also eager to reassure my family that I am well. Are you ready to sleep?" Ember asked with a yawn.

"Yes, Flame and Terrek wore me out." I smiled.

"I can smell that you are changing. You did enjoy yourself. I feel bad for taking you away from your family time. My anxiety has me selfish." Ember said softly.

"This is the least I can do for you, Ember. Let's get some sleep and see if we can figure out the answers you need."

As soon as I hit the pillow, I barely felt Ember take my hand, and I was in my dream world. A white mist of fog pillowed around us. I looked to my left, and Ember was holding my hand.

"Don't let go," Ember said as Harmony broke through the cloud in front of us, her mate, the god Hecat at her side.

"Does my family know I am safe? Why would you take me without warning?" Ember went right for it with Harmony.

I liked this about her, she never seems timid, just says it like she feels it.

"My dear Ember, I did not take you. My mother, the Goddess of true mating, took you. If I had known, I would have prepared everyone. I am working to remedy this. I will make a permanent portal on Laverian to allow you to go to and from your home on my planet Harmony to your family on Laverian."

"What? This makes no sense. I have no mate on Laverian." Ember said, completely confused.

"Your mother knows you are safe. I have been busy calming your parents, aunt, and uncle. Everyone has been using visions and the enchantment book to contact me. I am in a realm that is not of either universe, so my ability to communicate back in time has had my head spinning. Hecat has been guiding me."

"Yes, my Harmony loves you all so dearly. If she is concerned, it is my priority to do what makes my Harmony happy," Hecat said proudly.

"I am so proud of you, Darah, you fought well, and now you can build the life you dreamed of. My Hecat and I will establish a barrier to help protect our universe from Kane's. You have Babies in your future." The Goddess said with excitement. My mom and dad walked through the mist to join us.

Darah, we worried about you when we saw that battle. Oh, my heart, I am so glad to see you safe and whole.» My mother hugged me even though I held tight to Ember.

"Mom, Dad, meet Ember. She is my friend."

My dad pulled Ember into his big country arms. "Darlin, welcome to the family."

Ember held my hand and looked at me, perplexed.

"Thank you for protecting our Darah and her family, Ember. I always wanted another daughter. Now I have two more: you and Flame. I couldn't be more tickled pink." My mom said.

"Uhm, Mom, Dad, Ember is not my wife, uh, mate, I mean." I looked at Ember to see if I had missed a connection.

"Do you feel drawn to me like that? Cause I only feel sisterhood towards you." I asked Ember.

"Nope! Definitely, No sexual attraction on my part to you or your mates." Ember said with a shrug.

"We haven't explained that yet," Hecat interjected.

"I like to let these things happen naturally. It's so fun to watch." Harmony said.

"Jason, please join us," Harmony called. My brother came through the cloud.

"Jason," I said, holding my free arm out for a hug. But he ignored me. His eyes were locked onto Embers.

"What is happening?" I asked as the two stared at each other in a trance.

"They are imprinting as true mates, Darah."

When the moment passed, Ember sank to her knees, taking me with her as I held on tight to her hand.

"How can this be? He is dead. How will we be together?" Ember cried.

Jason ran to us and hugged her, "Ember, I will find a way." He promised.

Suddenly, my little brother seemed so grown up.

"Ember and Jason?" I asked, looking up at Harmony. My emotions felt every bit of sadness from Ember that she could not be with my brother as her destined mate.

"This is cruel for both of them. They deserve happiness just as I have found." I snapped, looking at the two gods for answers.

"Darah, I will re-birth Jason into my Eden as a phoenix. This will allow him to retain his memories and mate Ember as a grown male instead of being born as an infant."

Ember was squeezing my hand as she cried into Jason's neck. Seeing her vulnerable had my heart twisted up. She was usually so formidable and fierce.

"You can do this?" I asked, "Bring my family back to life?"

"Darlin, your mother and I are going to stay here. We like watching over you. Now, we can watch over Jason and Ember. The Gods are making an exception for Jason. We don't want to prevent that. We are grateful." My Dad said, smiling at me.

Jason cupped Ember's cheeks in his hands. He stared lovingly into her purple eyes.

"I am coming to you soon." He promised, and then he kissed her deeply.

This was weird for me as Ember tried to release my hand and wrap both her arms around my brother.

The two of them were oblivious to the rest of us. I pulled at her hand. I didn't want to be that close to my brother making out.

I sat there staring up at my parents and the two Gods. I realized my brother would live again and be with Ember. My heart swelled with happy emotions, and I started to tear up.

"Thank your mother for me, Harmony. My brother deserves this second chance at life." Ember successfully yanked her hand from mine, and we woke up in her bed.

"No, I just wanted to hold him." Ember cried as we sat up. She hugged me, sobbing.

CHAPTER 27

Darah

"Ember, I am sorry you had to meet like that, but I am so happy for you and my brother. He is the best! He deserves to live. I am glad he will have you."

We hugged each other and just cried. I could not imagine imprinting just to be separated moments later. Candy jumped on the bed to lay over our laps, licking us both frantically. He knew something was sad for us and wanted to fix this.

"It will be okay Ember. We will get you home, and my brother Jason will find his way to you soon."

I rubbed her back, trying to soothe her. Our wrist alarms broke us apart. Ember took a deep, calming breath.

"Thank you, Darah. I was worrying about my family, and now I have a new mate with a new extended Family. It was hard to imprint just to be separated. That is not natural for my kind." Ember spoke with emotion as she wiped a stray tear off her cheeks.

"Honey, we are gonna get you home, and you will have your side of the family and our side of the family celebrating you and Jason. We need something great like this to celebrate after everything we have gone through. I am happy to call you, my sister."

"Darah, there are no sides. We are all family now. Thank you for supporting me."

"You're right, Ember. One huge family now." I couldn't help but radiate happiness.

"These communication things are so intrusive. Ember said as she tapped at her device. We use the mind push to communicate long distances in my world. You, people, need some magic in your life instead of machines."

I laughed. "Don't I wish I could be magical? You are spectacular, Ember. Jason is lucky to have you."

"Thank you, Darah. Tell me what this means?" pointing at her wrist device.

"It means we are arriving at Laverian and must report to Flame five minutes ago. I guess there's no time for tea." I said as I grabbed my charred backpack and guitar to rush and meet Flame.

Candy and Flame kept pace with me as I entered the docking port of the medical city vessel that transported us to Laverian. Guards, let us pass per Flames orders.

I ran to my Flame and jumped in her arms, landing a sweet kiss. I knew it was incredibly unprofessional, and I should save this type of stuff for privacy. I needed to love my mates after such an emotional experience. Flame kissed me back and held me tight, not bothered by our audience.

"I am happy to see you too, my love." Flame said.

Gods, I love her sultry red eyes. She gave me and Terrek a particular gaze that radiated her love.

"Where's that purple demon man of mine?" I asked, searching for Terrek.

He is checking on his mother. A jump ship just landed here from the other carrier to reunite them. I did not want to meet her without you with me. He will get us when they are ready to go to the surface. I have his relatives prepared to go in that ship over there."

Flame pointed out a small jump ship that was waiting to launch. Her sad eyes said she felt terrible for what the enslaved people had endured.

"Flame, you did well. We saved them. Now we can all heal together."

I hugged her tightly. Candy rubbed his head up against her thigh, saying hello.

"Flame, meet our new sister Ember," I said playfully, explaining my dream encounter with the Goddess and my family.

"Welcome to the family, Ember. I am so glad we are more than friends." Flame said as she put her fist over her heart and bowed, giving Ember a warrior salute.

"Thank you, Flame. I am glad, too," Ember said.

Terrek came around the corner of the jump ship. As he saw us, he smiled, his black eyes smoldering. I ran to him and jumped in his arm, greeting him with a kiss.

"Mmmn, that's my girl." He moaned as he reluctantly let me slip down his body to stand on my feet.

Flame leaned up to kiss him briefly, "How is your mother?" she asked.

I stepped back so he could tell us. His gaze went sad just briefly.

It is so good to see her. She is frail, though. They tried to assimilate my mother, who is not controllable, so she suffered.

We cried over losing my father. She is still sad but pleased to be home and thrilled that I am alive. She wants to meet you both. Shall we?"

Terrek held his hand out in a wave, gesturing for us to board the ship to meet his mother.

"I am so sorry about your father, Terrek. I know it must be hard to stay stoic."

I grabbed his hand and said, "I am eager to meet your mother."

"I hope she likes me." Flame said, taking his other hand.

"She will love you, Flame. She will love you both." Terrek said.

"What's not to love, Flame? You are badass." I tried to reassure her.

My nervous energy flared up as I felt Flame's anxiety, my fingers entangled with hers. Terrek's sadness radiated backward toward us as he walked with a small limp in front of us.

My mates need to be well and loved. I reached my free hand out to rub his back in the only way I could give him support. I will love them always. I wish I were enough to keep all their pain and worries away. Reality can really suck at times.

After feeling the emotions from my brother and Ember imprinting and then being separated. Now that I was awake, we were about to meet Terrek's mother in the aftermath of war. My emotions were all over the place.

I would be strong for everyone. I must be. Flame said she found his mother but she was not in the best of health. Terrek was hiding his grief well, for our sake. He was so protective. We all were of each other.

We entered the jump ship and found Terrek's mother, Tora, sitting in a chair with a blanket on her lap. We got to have this meeting privately. Flame thought of everything. She was truly unique.

Terrek bent over and kissed his mom on the top of her head. He kneeled on the grated floor and held his mother's hand.

"Mom, with great pride, I introduce you to my true mates. This is Darah of Earth and Flame of Gia's.

"Flame, this is my mother, Tora of Laverian." Flame stepped forward and bowed with her fist over her heart in her warrior greeting.

"I am so happy to meet you, Mother Tora." Flame said.

"Flame, look at you, such a beauty! My son is blessed indeed. Please come hug me."

Toro lifted her shaky arms. She was so frail that I was

affected by the sight of her in that state. I received genuine love from Tora. The moment Flame leaned down to hug Tora. Her anxiety melted away. This was beautiful.

The frail, sickly woman transformed before me into a strong matriarch presence. Flame had not discussed her family much. Clearly, she prioritizes family as she melts into Tora's gentle hug. I loved this about her. We will need to meet all of her family next.

Flame stood with a sweet smile. She turned to me, and I smiled as I moved forward.

"Darah, you are such a beauty as well." Tora held her arms open for me. I hugged her and felt her acceptance and love. I felt her illness, too; she was strong for us, but she was very ill.

"I am so glad you are with us now. I feel so lucky to be a part of this family."

"My sweet child, our lives are saved, we have been returned home, and we have hope now. You made all this possible. You, Terrek, and Flame have saved us all. We are truly the lucky ones." Tora insisted, her voice frail.

"All my favorite ladies are with me. Let me take you home now," Terrek said genuinely.

I sat next to Tora as Flame and Terrek allowed the medical team to enter the ship so Tora could get her medical attention, and Flame launched, taking us home.

She planned for us to be the first to land. My heart was so whole and happy. My anxiety lingered, though. I worried for Tora. She was being humble and sweet. However, I sensed she was suffering greatly.

Flame landed just outside Terrek's village. I had only glimpsed his home in his projected memory when he was in the worthy machine. When I stepped outside and saw his house, I was breathless.

The deserted village was eerily empty. His home was well-made and beautifully beckoning. The smell of this land was refreshing, and the sense of being at home was simply wonderful. While this world lacks advanced technology, these homes were built with stunning craftsmanship.

"Come see our home. This one is my home next to my parents' home. The Chief house is my parent's or was . . . I suppose now our house is the Chief's house."

Terrek gave his mother a sweet glance as he offered to assist the medical team in escorting his mother off the ship.

"Mom, we are home now."

"Indeed, Son, I am happy to have returned home."

"We should take your mom home first. Get her settled." Flame insisted.

"These houses are so beautiful. Terrek, I am happy for all of us to be home." I said as we walked behind Tora and the team.

The moment we entered Tora's home, Terrek sat with his mother on a couch sitting area. He held his mom as she silently cried.

"I never thought I would see my home again. I can feel the difference in the air with your father gone now. Take your new bride's home and celebrate together. I need some rest and want to say a private farewell to your father in my home."

Tora was helped up, and she waved us off, insisting that her help would get her to her room without us. Her fatigue, Terrek's sadness for his mother, and his grief. It was so overwhelming. Terrek insisted on helping his mother.

Flame's concern for them both shown in her eyes. I saw the wheels turning. She plans on making this her next priority. I planned on helping her. The earth tones and wood walls made the inside of this home cozy and had a cabin style.

"Come step outside with me." I pulled on Flame's elbow. She would learn how stubborn I could be when I insisted on helping her ease the load. She was always taking on too much by herself.

"Okay, I can use some fresh air. Laverian has very crisp air. I will enjoy it here." Flame said. Terrek stepped outside.

"My mates are you ready to see our home?" he asked.

Terrek took our hands and walked us to the house across the path to his chief house, our home now. The moment we entered. I knew I was home. Very detailed hand-crafted wood lined the walls, and sturdy furniture was made of the same wood style and upholstered with rustic patterns.

I looked around and saw a spacious seating area with a tiled fireplace. I just wanted to fill this home with our babies. The big open window that overlooked the center of the village and the tall trees made into a gate kept the wild out. Gave us the best view, I pictured our future children running and playing. This was my happily ever after.

We were happy together and eager for a proper home welcoming between us, but we were all keen to start the homecoming of the Laverian people and refugees who chose to live here after the rescue.

The Galactic Empire's resources allowed us to help everyone reasonably smoothly.

Ember and Candy came down in the second wave of transit jumper ships.

After everything settled for the night, we returned home to the Chief's house. Ember and Candy slept in one of the many spare bedrooms. I kissed my sweetheart's good night as I was exhausted and fell asleep fast.

CHAPTER 28

Flame

My implants had given me a stigma among my people. I was constantly proving that I was capable and strong, stronger than most. I felt no shame with my mates; they loved me wholly, and I think they were amazing.

Both Terrek and Darah kissed my markings whenever I got naked around them. More and more, I was starting to accept these implants as a beautiful accessory rather than my scars.

I was so in love. For the first time in my life, I could enjoy life, and my goals were no longer being the best of the warriors to make my mother proud.

I had found all I wanted was for these two souls to be happy and loved. I would be the best for both of them and the family we would build together.

Ember was eager to go home to Harmony's planet. My soldiers reported an anomaly on the surface of the planet. The scanning satellites picked it up. The Frio spacemen have completed the shield around the planet, and the entry port was almost finished.

Satellites scanned the surface of the planet, the airspace, and outer space for any anomalies or threats. I got my approval for commanding the Galactic Empire forces stationed on Laverian.

I had Ember, Darah, and Candy with me. Terrek was still busy greeting his people and speaking with his elder advisers about the transition of his Chief role and as the new Laverian Emperor. He had proudly got his tattoo marking for Chief completed today. Another reason I feel so comfortable here on Laverian tattoo markings are common.

We landed the jumper in a break of the forest, a small meadow. As we walked to the anomaly's source, Candy ran. He was happy to be home too.

There was a chetaht pride released near here. I had a feeling he was going to greet his kind.

"Stay close by boy, or you might get lost," Darah yelled after him.

"I think he will find his way back to you, no matter how far he runs. Besides, my scans can find him if he gets lost," I promised.

"What in the world?" Darah said as we stepped in front of a big tree with a red door and a crystal nob placed oddly in the thick tree trunk.

"Yes! That is a God portal door. It looks like the one on Harmony's planet, my home. Only our door is blue." Ember said excitedly.

"I had to be sucked through a pond, and you got a door. Some girls get all the luck," Darah said playfully.

I walked to the door and tried to open it, but it would not budge an inch.

"How does it work?"

"Back home, we write in an enchanted book and knock three times. I don't know how it will work to travel through. We only ever received things, and people through our door.

No one ever left until I was sucked into it to be taken up

here. Harmony said the portal will allow us to go both ways now." Ember said as she approached the door.

"Darah, if this works and I go home, I promise I will bring Jason here as soon as I reunite with him, and we complete our bond. I will bring my family here to meet you all. I hope you will also come to visit us." Ember promised.

"Ember, you saved my mates, helped us fight the Kanenites, and saved all these people. I am so happy you and my brother have each other. I can't wait to see him, so bring him here as soon as possible. We will visit ya'll too, as soon as we get things settled here." Darah gave Ember a tight hug.

"Ember, my new sister, travel well and return to us as often as you can. We will come to visit you as well. Besides, I can't wait to see your magical world," I said, giving Ember my fist salute and a tight hug.

Candy jumped up on Ember and licked her chin.

"I am going to miss you too, my furry friend. You keep my family safe while I am away, okay, boy?" Ember said, her eyes tearing up.

She stepped to the door and knocked three times. The door opened, and a darkness so black filled the doorway. Ember stepped in and disappeared in the blackness. The door slammed shut. Just like that, Ember was gone. I pulled Darah in for a hug, her eyes tearing up as Ember left.

"My little earthling, I am so happy for our new sister, I am looking forward to meeting your brother Jason. I have never met a resurrected soul before. We are truly blessed."

"I know, I don't think I will believe it until I hug him in real life."

I kissed my sweet southern Darah, distracting her from her tears.

"I am just emotional, with this pregnancy, I can't stop my tears," Darah said.

My heart momentarily stopped.

"So, the seal worked? We are having a baby girl?" I asked, hoping this was true.

"I woke up and ran to the bathroom to throw up. I used the medical device to scan my body just to get a diagnosis and something to ease my upset stomach. It confirmed my pregnancy. Babe, I am officially the first Earthling to have gotten pregnant by a female. Congratulations we are soon to be moms!" Darah kissed me through happy tears.

"I would like to name her Spark if you and Terrek agree?" Darah said.

I started to tear up, "My mother, Zion, will be so proud to have a grandbaby named after my birthing mom, Spark. I wish I could have known her. I am hopeful Terrek will be thrilled for a baby girl named Spark." I said choked up.

I was so happy tonight. I would prepare a special dinner to celebrate, and I would share my news of conceiving twins. An egg from Darah has been implanted, and my egg took Terrek's seed successfully.

Three babies in our future. We flew back to our village, where we gathered supplies for our dinner. I cooked the rest of the afternoon away.

"I am sorry I missed seeing Ember off today, I did say farewell this morning. Wow! look at this spread." Terrek said as he entered our dining area to greet Darah and me.

"Hello, my sexy male, I like the way your markings turned out," I said as I hugged him to kiss him sweetly.

They filled up his right arm and curved across his shoulder, the tribal lines highlighted the bulge of his muscles.

"I am one lucky gal to have two tatted-up lovers. Damn, your so sexy." Darah said as she kissed him.

I prepared a meal to celebrate, we have some good news." I said waving my hand for us to sit.

"Smells delicious; I am all for good news," Terrek said as he sat to eat.

"Darah has news too, but I want to tell you both something first."

"What is it, my love? Terrek's sexy black eyes looked at me with affection.

"I am pregnant by both of you, were having twins!"

Terrek dropped his fork, stood from the table, and picked me up, twirling us in a circle. His happiness radiated in joyous laughter.

"Yes! This is the best news ever!" He proclaimed.

Darah started weeping, full-on sobbing.

"Darah, love are you okay?" I asked as Terrek and I broke apart to check on her.

"It's just I am so happy, and these pregnancy hormones make me cry over everything." she cried.

"You are pregnant too?" Terrek pulled her up in his arms.

"Oh, Darah, I am so happy, you two have made me a father."

EPILOGUE

Darah

One year later

I had convinced Terrek and Flame that we needed our own version of Christmas. My favorite time of year was celebrating, exchanging gifts, and having family time. They thought it was a great way to implement an Earth custom for our children and to mark the year anniversary of our return home.

We call it gift exchange day. I popped seeds resembling corn and Flame and strung them together. We made ornaments from the palm nuts that fell from the trees. I commissioned a potter to make stars and moon-shaped clay ornaments. We used a large fern to decorate our seating area. I wrapped the gifts with scarves, and the lady at the market hand-dyed them with certain Laverian roots and flowers.

The Laverian people have adapted to the upgrade in technology, and they adored Terrek as their leader. They saw Flame as their savior and brought her gifts of gratitude.

Everyone was praising and adoring our babies. We were

constantly offered help for taking care of them. Every woman here was an auntie or a grandmother to our children. The whole village was one big family.

My momma would say, "It takes a village to raise babies."

Electricity and all had been established, our sun provides the power for all our needs.

This was better than any Christmas tree I ever had before. I was so excited to see our babies each year have these traditions. Terrek sat in his big rocker, holding all three babies. Little Spark looked so much like Flame, her red eyes so alert and wise in her baby face.

Flame had her babies three weeks after I gave birth to Spark. Her gestation took longer than Earth females. A tiny purple male that looked like Terrek with Flame's red eyes. His little horn nubs were adorable. We named him John Tak after both my father and Terrek's.

His twin sister looks like me with blue eyes. We named her Dana, after my mother. Mother Zion had taken leave to help us with the babies. Mother Tora had recovered fully and was no longer frail.

The two grandmothers doted over our babies. I wished my mom was here, but she came to me in my dreams. She visits the babies while they sleep. Flame hugged me from behind. We stood there watching our little family as Terrek held our babies.

"He is the best father." Flame spoke in my ear. Sending gooseflesh down my arms.

I turned my head back to kiss her. "Yes, we are living the dream."

The knock on the door disrupted our moment. Candy growled his hackles up. Now that we had babies, he was extremely protective.

"Candy, be nice. No one will harm our babies," I said as I swung open the door.

I nearly fainted when my brother's smiling face filled my doorframe.

"Jason!" I jumped in his open arms.

"Darah, I had to come meet my nieces and nephew. I brought gifts."

Ember came in behind Jason, holding bags of gifts in her hands. Flame grabbed some bags as more people stepped into our home.

Zion took Candy to another room just as a precaution.

"Darah, meet the in-laws," Jason said.

"This is my mother-in-law Kayla the Dragoon Queen; she was from Earth once too."

"I am so happy to meet you, finally, Darah." Kayla pulled me in for a brief hug.

"This is my father-in-law, Talen the Dragoon King." Jason introduced him to me. Talen nodded with his arms full of wrapped gifts.

"Glad to be here." He said, his dark purple eyes gazing at me.

I had to convinced Aunt Brooke and Uncle Fang to stay behind on harmony, I didn't want to overwhelm y'all." Jason said joyously.

My heart was full as tears fell, happy tears. I had come a long way from a poor ranch hands daughter who wanted to attend college and make my parents proud.

Terrek and Flame stood proudly beside me as we watched our new family dote over our babies. I leaned to kiss Terrek and then Flame.

"I love you both with all my heart. This is my happy ever after." I said in complete happiness.

Flame, Terrek and I told our story to Jason's new family and our life felt completely happy and full of love.

The end, for now.

About the Author

TANYA STEVERDING lives in east Texas, where she enjoys spending time with her family and her beloved grandchildren. When she is not writing, she is crafting or painting. She is also an avid reader and fan of paranormal romance and the young adult genre.

Tanya enjoys traveling in her RV and bringing her pack of toy poodles everywhere.

Creating worlds of Fantasy/ Sci-fi and Paranormal Romance for her readers has been her dream come true.

HARMONY
Interference

by

Tanya Steverding

https://linktr.ee/tanyasteverding